I0645062

Tony was used to doing the investigating, not being investigated, and he didn't like it one bit...

"That's enough," Tony said. "I've had it. I am getting out of this chair and exiting the room and the building unless you arrest me. And, if you want to arrest me, I'll call my PBA rep and the lawyer from the PBA. Then it will get really ugly. Soooooo, bye-bye, guys."

"Sit down, asshole. You'll leave when we are through with you. Not before."

Tony began to rise, Kelly moved to put his hand on Tony's shoulder.

"If you touch me, you rotten fuck, I'll drop you where you stand. Then I'll shove the leg of this chair up your ass. This is my house. You are an uninvited guest."

Captain Brainerd's entrance was like a bucket of cold water dumped on angry dogs. Silence and stares all around. His demeanor screamed authority.

"Tony, let's grab lunch. Sorry I can't invite you boys, but my budget is tight."

Brainerd wrapped his arm around Tony's shoulders. The uncle escorted the interviewee to the safety of the captain's office. The skunks skulked from the precinct.

Detective First Grade Tony Sattill of the NYPD is assigned the crime scene investigation of the gruesome, ritualistic "Handyman Murders." Once the case is turned over to the homicide detectives, Tony is asked to dig into the past of fellow Detective, Elija Washington. Tony uncovers uncommonly large cash flows in Elija's past and a possible major cover-up by NYPD, but then the evidence in the Handyman case begins to incriminate Tony. Lab tests reveal a link between him and the murders, and he knew all the victims. Tony's world is crashing in on him while, all around him, close friends are dying. Is Tony pegged to be the fall guy—or just the next victim?

KUDOS for *Hidden Agenda*

In *Hidden Agenda* by John Andes, Tony Satill is an NYPD crime-scene detective. When he is asked to dig into the activities of a fellow detective, things start to go bad for Tony. His friends start dying, and he becomes the person of interest in the murders. Now he has to do some fancy footwork in order to find the real killer and save himself, not to mention his career. With the help of his friend and attorney, Franklin, Tony digs for the truth, but what he uncovers may be worse than losing his career. It may cost him his life. Well written, fast paced, and down-to-earth, the story will not only catch and hold your interest, it will keep you guessing until the end. ~ *Taylor Jones, The Review Team of Taylor Jones & Regan Murphy*

Hidden Agenda by John Andes is the story of Tony Sattill, a detective for the NYPD. Tony is called to the scene of a murder—his friend Charlotte Jenks—and things begin to go downhill from there. Once the case is handed over to the homicide detectives, Tony is assigned to investigate a colleague who is suspected of not properly investigating a bank case. Tony discovers that not only was the bank case closed too soon, but it hints of corruption at the highest levels. But before he can report his findings, he discovers he is a suspect in Charlotte's murder. He knows he is being framed, but by who, what for, and how does he prove it? Written in a unique voice, filled with great characters, fast paced, and gritty, *Hidden Agenda* will keep you glued to your seat, turning pages as fast as you can—a mystery you can really sink your teeth into. ~ *Regan Murphy, The Review Team of Taylor Jones & Regan Murphy*

HIDDEN AGENDA

JOHN ANDES

A Black Opal Books Publication

GENRE: MYSTERY-DETECTIVE/CRIME THRILLER

This is a work of fiction. Names, places, characters and incidents are either the product of the author's imagination or are used fictitiously, and any resemblance to any actual persons, living or dead, businesses, organizations, events or locales is entirely coincidental. All trademarks, service marks, registered trademarks, and registered service marks are the property of their respective owners and are used herein for identification purposes only. The publisher does not have any control over or assume any responsibility for author or third-party websites or their contents.

HIDDEN AGENDA
Copyright © 2017 by John Andes
Cover Design by Jackson Cover Designs
All cover art copyright © 2017
All Rights Reserved
Print ISBN: 978-1-626948-19-8

First Publication: DECEMBER 2017

Published by Black Opal Books **http://www.blackopalbooks.com**

Dedicated to P.B.M.

Because it is a lie, a hidden agenda separates people.
If someone lives by hidden agendas,
separation is absolute.
This is sin.

PROLOGUE

Who are you?"

In a world of former lives and changing partners, do we ever really know? Beneath a very beautiful stone can be the home of a snake. Beneath a discolored moss-covered shard can be gold. Where have all the good men gone and where are all the gods? Where has all the honesty gone?

Our parents work hard to keep alive the heart of integrity. In my youth, life mirrored the turn of the century and Great Depression attitudes inculcated by my grandparents into my parents. Work hard. Save. Be clean, somber, and sober. Feed, clothe, and protect the children. Then the next Great War came and went. Morals and mores were distorted by the war effort. The economy expanded so rapidly, anything was possible, and we wanted it all. More education. Bigger houses and cars. Much,

much more money. More free time to enjoy the fruits of our labors. The world's endless possibilities grew beyond our wildest dreams. Each generation wanted more. More religion. More assurance of peace and tranquility. More ways to escape. Booze, drugs, and out-in-the-open intimacy ruled. Money became God.

Some people succeed. Some people stumble. Some people fall from grace. Some of these are reborn into new worlds, new faces, lives, and lifestyles. But they have to pay for this rebirth. Nothing comes without a price. Leave home. Leave family. Sacrifice others. Those who are sacrificed seek not balance, but retribution. Everyone has a hidden agenda. We just don't know what's on the list.

CHAPTER 1

1204 Lexington Avenue:

She drowned. Drowned in her own blood. Probably took the better part of an hour. She couldn't fight against it. Never shook her head. No blood splatters on the wall or floor. Why? The caked blood from her nose to her nipples indicates she tried to blow the blood from her lungs, but her mouth was taped shut side to side and top to bottom. The tape wrapped around her neck was like a collar and affixed to the wall. It was intentionally loose so as not to choke, yet it was secure enough so that the vic could not escape. True sadistic torture. Eyes wide open so she could see. Seeing, but not being able to do anything, was its own fear. Pain without the tormentor to which the victim could respond. It must have been hell. Slowly swallowing her death, all the while trying to breathe. Trying to exhale death and inhale life at the same time. Impossible.

"The absence of tape burns on her wrists confirms there was no struggle. My guess is that she's been dead between twelve and twenty-four hours. The accurate determination is better left to the rats in the lab. There is nothing sexy about a blood-covered, nude female. NYPD Crime Analysis Team is halfway through its on-site investigation."

Each CAT included a lead detective, a uniform, and two members from the Scientific and Technical Analysis Group. The STAGs were the lab rats, techies, and near-meds. Each borough had three CATs. CAT was the brainchild of some committee downtown at One Police Plaza and was designed to train up-and-coming force members with actual crime scene procedure and analysis, as well as take the burden of initial data gathering off the shoulders of the investigative force. Each CAT was headed by a young detective selected after rigorous psychological testing. Selected on the basis that the detective had all the right tools for command decisions and the gift. The gift of deep comprehension, for seeing the little details and their connectors that abounded or for sensing what was missing or what did not fit. For grasping what *probably* happened at a crime scene. Not the why, but the what.

The lead detective was not a glamorous profiler. He was just a very observant, intelligent, and sensitive individual. CAT operated only in non-immediate violent crime situations—deaths, which were over twelve hours old. The trail of the perp was cold. CAT replaced the two detectives, four uniforms, and a complete Crime Scene Unit in cold situations only. Most calls for CAT came directly to the precinct and not through nine-one-one.

Veteran detectives called it the Cold Asshole Team or the Pussy Squad. If it was not an emergency, give it to the pussycats. They hated it because they thought it took the entire process of old-fashioned detective work away from the ill-fitting suits. What they really objected to was that it was the crest of the wave of the future, wherein there would be greater specialization and greater reliance on awareness and sensitivity and less on legwork and the third degree.

The future, according to the seers and knowers, would be one of modularity. Each module would be connected by and interlinked to each other and the precincts, and precincts would be interlinked to each other via the citywide computer system. The entire plan was quite simple and very efficient. CAT was assembled and sent, based on who was up, who was available from the various disciplines. A roster was kept in the NYPD main computer system and could be tapped by any precinct captain or shift commander. Often the team would be comprised of members who were not from the same precinct. The CATs were sent borough-wide and not beholden to an individual precinct. The team went to the cold scene, gathered all the pertinent information, spent time walking and looking at the scene from all angles, made observations, drew vague conclusions, and issued hypotheses. All in the prescribed format, CAT 1221. The four members spoke into personal digital-recorders at the scene. Later, they downloaded electronic blips into networked laptops, so they could read each other's findings and observations.

It was up to the team leader—in this case, Detective First Grade Tony Sattill—to merge and purge the information, infuse his hypotheses, and develop a single comprehensive report on the murder scene. This report along with the coroner's report was turned over to the investigating detectives within twenty-four hours of the on-site analysis. Addenda from anyone other than the medical examiner's office were considered a sign of shoddy work on the part of the CAT leader. An addendum was considered an error by the older detectives and corroborated their view that CAT was worthless.

Sattill was a veteran of the force and one of its soon-to-be powerful. Minor excursions into the lands of alcohol and Colombian Candy held up his advancement, but he had repaid his dues five-fold. He also had a Dutch Uncle or godfather on the force. Now he was ready to move up. When promoted, he would oversee the CATs in Manhattan. When the old man was ready to be transitioned to One Police Plaza, Tony and two others would be in line to move into a single spot. Like musical chairs: three dancers and one chair. He had worked his butt off and introduced as much technology as the old dinosaur could understand. When Tony took over, new technology could be introduced to all field trips, not just in his borough. Only JJ Rierdan and Elija Washington could sit in what would be Tony's chair."

Tony continued walking, staring, and talking. Stalking an absent killer who stalked the victim. Tony tried to take the exact steps, make the exact moves of the killer, who was long gone from the scene.

"Well, he is really sick. Bobby, don't miss the dried goo on her knees. It looks like it could be semen. Maybe the perp did her up, did her, and did her in. I wonder if he fucked her before he stuck the instrument in her throat. My guess is an ice pick or something very similar. Or, maybe he stabbed her as he came *a la de Sade*. Before or after? Carefully examine the wrists. Wrists taped, the tape was folded into a flap of numerous layers, and then the flap was nailed to the wall. Extra-long roofing nails. Ones that won't pull out or tear the tape. The guy must have used a full roll of duct tape. His work reflects handyman talents. Took his time. Yet he experienced passion and fucked her. Or, at least, he came on her.

"The ice pick was driven in at the proper angle to pierce the artery and let the blood run down the throat and not out the entry wound. Only one wound. He knew where, how, and why it would work. This guy is a pro or a really torqued psycho. There are no fingerprints in the blood. But there is a cigarette butt. It's a Doral. Snuffed out by hand on the wall, not on her, and dropped near her left foot. Did he smoke before or after the murder? He is not afraid to mark his territory. Why? Why the left foot? Is he sure we can't find him?

"Tell the detectives to check FBI files and look for MOs that match. DNA analysis won't be back from the labs for thirty-six hours."

Recorder entry over, Tony hovered over the body. "Did anyone find an ice pick?"

The question earned a resounding silence from everyone.

"Bobby. Morris. Make sure you download your tapes before seven. I want to work on this tonight and tomorrow. Please tell Doctor Cut Up that this case is special. I need an interim report by eleven tonight and her complete report no later than Saturday noon. She will have to work OT. I'll authorize the time and charges. This is front page, leading, bleeding news. There will be hell to pay come Sunday if we don't have a ton of real information for our friends, the wrinkled-shirt, donut-scarfing detectives. It's okay to cut her down, bag her, and call the meat wagon."

The room was a bloody mess. Charlotte Jenks was dead. Why? Who? No one at the scene realized that Tony knew Charlotte. No one knew they shared a summerhouse with six other people. Charlotte was the bed-sharing friend of Bill Davis. Also in the house were Tony's lover, Connie Wilhaus; Dan and Mildred Bren; and the Saylors, Red and Babs. This tenuous, behind-the-scenes relationship between Tony and the deceased must never get into the public light. Otherwise, he would have to take heat from people with nothing better to do. Or simply removed from the case to avoid the appearance of impropriety. Too many questions. Too little information. No one must know. No one.

Tony had a sense that this MO would not be found in anyone's files. Like sensing something was about to come out of the shadows and strike him, Tony felt he was going to see a repeat of this carnage before too long. This event was just the beginning. He never had this sense before, but he had never seen a non-police friend as a victim. *Was it Charlotte or was it the scene? How long before it happens again? When? How to stop it before it happens?*

Tony's personal life had always been separate from his day job. The other members of CAT thought he was just another college boy, like Rierdan and Washington— too fancy for the pubs after the shift and too busy for the weekend cookouts in Queens or Brooklyn. He had his own circle of friends, old college chums. These friends knew he worked for the NYPD in some arcane capacity. They never probed for facts. That wouldn't be proper according to the Code of Non-intrusion to which the graduates of The Ancient Eight strictly adhered. Tony lived two lives, not unlike James Philbrick. The spheres were separate because that's what Tony wanted.

Fridays from the first of May to the end of September, Tony's non-police-force friends shared a beach house in Mantoloking on the Jersey shore. It had been this way for years. Every Friday evening, four couples raced from their respective homes in metropolitan New York to The Bluffs, the name of the shore house. The race was more like a road rally: specific times for specific distances. Everyone knew the exact distance from their abodes to The Bluffs. So, requiring an average speed of sixty miles per hour, precise ETAs had been established for each couple.

Tony and Connie traveled from 60 East Ninety-Sixth Street in Manhattan, a trip of eighty-two miles or one hour and twenty-two minutes. The Brens lived at 145 Nutley Boulevard in Montclair, New Jersey. Their trip was seventy-one minutes. The Saylors traveled eighty-eight minutes from sixteen Laymon Court in Englewood, New Jersey. Bill and Charlotte left from either her house in Brooklyn or his co-op at the tip of Manhattan Island. Their trip was either eighty or seventy-four minutes. To meet the benchmarks, the competitors had to fight through city or suburban traffic with all the lights and gridlocks of Fridays. Then speed at eighty-five-plus miles per hour on the New Jersey Turnpike and Garden State Parkway to compensate for any previously lost time. And, there was always lost time prior to the Jersey Auto-bahns.

To keep everyone honest required that one of the members of each team call The Bluffs just as the team was starting the trip. The answering machine would rec-ord the date, time, and telephone number of the four calls. The teams would punch in at the house using the Zeit clock on the mantel. Punching the time clock gave them the feeling of working in a factory: a world they never knew. The clock was driven by satellite, which carried the time from Greenwich, England. The satellite was ca-pable of adjusting the time on the mantel clock if it ever wavered from the truth, as in electrical storms or outages. The eight had invested over $5,000 in the clock and tele-phone system. The telephone system included lines for eight discrete receivers.

Everyone worked over the weekend, for no other reason than to show the others how difficult was their lot in life.

To add interest to the road rally, each couple had to kick in $200 per weekend. Winner take all. The winning time had to be no more than fifteen seconds under the true allotted time—never over. And arrival had to be before ten, which meant that driving was done during the worst traffic on the East Coast. If no team won, the pot rolled over to the next weekend. A team could win or lose a maximum of $3,000 during the summer. But winning the money was not as important as beating the others.

The males of the group vaguely remembered each other from college. Some reconnected via former relationships, disconnected, then reconnected. There had not been a constant cohesion. Now there was a bond based on memories and faith in the inaccuracy of history. Time gaps meant there was always something new to tell. There were many life gyrations of emotional and economic *drunkalogs*. The eight were compatible, though occasionally aloof. The camaraderie forged in the economic, social, and academic furnace of Brown had long since cooled. New pressures from careers caused the chums to become self-protective and somewhat self-centered.

Police work was its own shield. Nobody really wanted to know the politics, shitty hours, violence, and the endless drudgery of details, forms, and CYA documents. Friends and neighbors, if they knew Tony was a cop, were interested only in the exhilaration and glamour of midnight raids on the drug houses and arrests of syndicate bosses. This was not Tony's world.

Who was Charlotte? Charlotte Jenks was a fabric designer. She was, as expected, constantly sketching and experimenting with colors and patterns. Having worked for three Fashion Avenue houses, she went out on her own a few years ago. Apparently made decent money, but the pressure to always be different and better was horrendous. She drank a little too much very expensive vodka. She drank too much very strong coffee. Took tranquilizers and mood elevators. Never seemed to eat much. A classic case of well-directed self-destruction. Yesterday, someone just beat her to her demise.

Bill Davis worked in the financial world. He was the liaison between his company and the mutual fund managers, who managed the portfolios in annuities and variable life insurance sold by the company. He had been with North American Financial Markets since B-school. He started at NAFM well before the big Bull market and rode the beast for all it was worth. The right place at the right time. Income was deep into the six figures. He had a bunch stashed in various instruments. He was set for life. Never married. Tony was never one-hundred-percent sure of Bill's heterosexuality. His mannerisms were vaguely foppish.

Tony shared a city residence with his girlfriend of the past few years, Connie Wilhaus. Connie had been a cheerleader at Penn State, and it showed. Vivacious and wholesome on the outside. Unfortunately though, moody and sometimes confrontational when she wanted something her own way. Connie was deep into physical fitness—the right nutrition, food, and supplements, proper exercise, and only a little drinking. Maybe a little too centered. But she was successful. One of the owners of a small chain of spas called The Seven Sisters. The spas catered to younger businesswomen or any female who could afford the steep membership fee and the extras that were always available; the latest in casual athletic clothes and accessories, group vacations, four-night hikes. No men allowed.

Dan and Mildred Bren were Amway distributors. They sold the right to buy from the catalog to those who sold the right to buy from the catalog. Regular meetings, extensive travel, and daily counseling down-line and up-line. Dan had been a detailer for a French drug firm. His territory was Metro New York to Boston. He met Millie at an Amway meeting. Instant love…or heat. Their combined enthusiasm and energy were natural strengths to make multi-level marketing successful. Plus, he had contacts with doctors, nurses, and hospital administrators. Married three years less than they had been in the business. The first for both. They now made enough to never work again, but they were driving to one more level for complete financial security. Security for their children and their children.

Saylor, Winfield and Baker, Inc. was a law firm founded by this generation's fathers. Randolph Edmonton Dalhousie "Red" Saylor IV was the partner aggressively pushing the firm into mergers and acquisitions. Barbara Stillington Winfield "Babs" was his bride of the ten years. Second marriage for both. Often, they were just "too cute for words." Children from previous unions lived with former spouses in Arizona and Pennsylvania, respectively. Red and Babs were talking about a new brood of the breed. But they loved the self-indulgences of money and no children—regular evening tennis, every-night dinners at the best restaurants or their clubs, and matching Mercedes convertibles that were never more than three years old. Babs brought as much money and emotional baggage into the relationship as Red. She constantly sniped at "her boy, Red" and aggressively flirted with beach boys and tennis pros—entitlements of her privileged status, she claimed after four drinks. Their presence at The Bluffs was a showy escape from everyday neighbors, who must rely on the Northern New Jersey Golf and Country Club for the summer weekends.

No race for Tony this weekend. He'd just forfeit his $200. Couldn't leave until well after ten, because of Charlotte's murder. This delay suited Connie. She had to meet with the accountant and money people to discuss the expansion plans for the chain. She pushed for a Saturday morning departure. She would come home when she was done with her work, and they could leave before seven. This allowed Tony to work until he fell asleep. By seven, all the files would be downloaded, and he could bug Dr. Cut Up at the NYPD Morgue by nine. The doctor would go through her usual flirt-attack routine on the telephone. These were the first two stages of the conquer-submit syndrome. The game always ended in a tie, because that's the way of office politics. Numerous times she thought she had won because that was the way of Tony's politics.

It was Friday, the unofficial holy day of purity-driven indulgence. He showered off the smell and dirt of death from Charlotte's apartment and started to prep dinner. The feast of sundown consisted of veal, pan seared in extra virgin olive oil, Chardonnay, shallots and capers, wild rice, and a salad of plum tomatoes, bean sprouts, hearts of lettuce and black olives: comfort food for the chosen. Two glasses of a '91 California Merlot cleansed the taste of death. Tony had saved some of the feast for Connie. The complete Hallelujah Chorus, compliments of the London Philharmonic, was playing at volume level fifteen. The fantastically energizing effort poured from eight speakers, filled every corner and space in the five rooms, and swabbed his ears of city noise and the pettiness of the day. The ritual complete, his personal space became quiet, or as quiet as can be expected from a fourth-floor loft on Friday night in the summer. Window air conditioners and industrial strength ceiling fans performed the dual functions of cooling and blocking the street noise. Dishes done, he settled into work. The roll-top desk and chair in his office were a gift from his brother after Tony's return to the clean and sober crowd. The set made a definitive statement about his new work values.

He was plugged into the NYPD system. The Fax was poised for spewing. He drew down the reports from the lab-rats, Bobby and Morris. They had worked together for the past couple of years and saw things slightly differently on each scene. Bobby tended to be theoretical, whereas Morris was flat out black-and-white. Combined, their reports gave a textural picture of the scene. The report from the uniform on the scene covered facts about the victim: address, name, lifestyle based on clothing in the closets, food in the kitchen, furniture, art, magazines, books, videos, etc. The uniform also took information from the super, who had gone into the apartment to check the pipes for a leak. He found the cold body and called the precinct. Tony read, cut and pasted into the appropriate boxes in form CAT 1221, accessible by the investigating detectives. If they wanted all of the backup, they could go to the shared files. Tony can't afford to miss any details. Any small deviation in the different reports must be noted because it could be critical to solving the case. Tony called Dr. Martha Minnig, a.k.a. Dr. Cut Up.

"Hello, Doctor, Detective Sattill here. I'm calling to determine your progress on the female victim brought into you earlier today. She was stabbed with an ice pick."

"Hello, Tony. I have nothing exciting or arcane yet. Yours was third in line as of two p.m. As of now, she's on the table. I'm about to start. I should have some dangerously sketchy knowledge for you in about two hours, say around eleven. Call back then."

Advantage Doctor. The edge in her voice signaled her awareness that she was being pushed and that she didn't like it. But she was the best cutter in the department. She worked at this seemingly thankless task because her father had. She could be Chief Medical Examiner of the five boroughs in a few years. Dr. Cut Up had a voice that could peel chrome off a bumper at fifty feet. That was intriguing to Tony. The good doctor was smart, held a position of power, was great at her job, and her voice turned him on. Tony wondered what she looked like. Was she as wonderfully sensuous and attractive as her voice hinted, or was she like Allison Steele? Steele was a late-night DJ on WNEW. She was known as the *Nightbird.* She would sexually intone free verse over the intro song to her gig. Her throatiness and the electro-sounds of the decade were seductive. In person, Allison was not what all the young men had hoped based on her voice.

Tony turned on the TV news to see if the vic had made the electronic medium. The longer she was out of the public eye, the longer the investigative detectives had to work their magic. *What about Bill? Does he know? He can't know as much as I know. Or, can he?* Thoughts bounced in his head like a dream. His nap was interrupted by Connie's entrance. The large metal door opens noisily on purpose.

"Hey, sweetie, how was your financial cluster-fuck? If you're hungry, the remains of the sacrificed veal and all the other goodies can be nuked. Would you like me to set your table?"

"That would be great. I want to shower. Is there any wine open?"

"A Merlot. I'll heat the meal and pour. You wash."

In fifteen minutes, she slinks into the kitchen wrapped in terry—head and body. She glides into a cush-ioned seat at the banquet before her on the oak table. Tony has poured two glasses of wine and opened a second bottle. Her dining experience lasts about ten minutes. She is famished. Waves her glass for more wine.

"Well, Detective First Grade Anthony William Sattill Jr., you are looking at an about-to-be very wealthy woman. Tonight, we decided to go public to fund the expansion of The Seven Sisters. My portion of the pie should be worth ten to twenty million dollars. My share of the retained stock will be worth the same and more when we go national or get eaten by a larger fish. All the details and final value have to be worked out over the next months. Money is in the wings. So, while the seven of us focus on becoming millionaires, we have to slowly relinquish the all the day-to-day crap to the managers. We will even launch an advertising campaign to create awareness in the buying public. I am so filled with facts and things to do that I can hardly speak. This much I know. I want a third glass of wine. I want to dry my hair. And I want to love you into spasms of exhaustion."

"That's super, sweetie. Beautiful, rich, and horny. Wow! A combination more powerful than I could have anticipated for tonight."

"But we can't tell anybody about the plans for The Seven Sisters. No one can know before our advisors are ready to leak the information. Fair deal?"

"Fair deal. Now you dry, and I'll clean up. Here, have another touch of the grape."

Ten rings at the Morgue mean that the good doctor is involved in her work. At this hour they're all in the cut-up room.

"You're twenty minutes late, Tony. Here's what I know. She was not in good health before she died. A lot of alcohol damage to her system. The balance of the chemical and tox screen will be available by tomorrow morning. Her last meal was a non-descript cereal. One ice pick puncture. She drowned in her own blood. Minor bruises on the wrists and ankles. No marks of a beating or violence. She was not penetrated. No tears or abrasions. The semen was deposited. None in the mouth. Interesting, the little soldiers lost their tails. They were not fresh when deposited. As if they were stored prior to arrival. Premeditation. And here is the kicker. She was pregnant. Tops, three months. Fetus died right after the mother. So far, here's what I guess. Whoever did this knew exactly what he was doing. And, therefore why. Was in her home, got her drunk, and sadistically killed her. It looks like he then tossed his sperm on her to show contempt for her. This is my best shrink-like guess. It's free, so it's worth what you paid. I'll input all the information in the shared files. You can retrieve it at your leisure by the ocean side. And, a *thank you* is insufficient. Good night."

Game to the good doctor.

CHAPTER 2

43 Ocean Drive:

Connie slept from Eighty-Sixth Street and Eighth Avenue until the Mazda 626 stopped beneath the large pine tree to the left of The Bluffs. The first two cars got the garage. The second two shielded their cars from the piercing sun by parking under the branches of an ancient, huge pine trees. Tony's twelve-year-old Mazda had been a workhorse. Long since paid for, the repair and maintenance bills were considered healthcare maintenance. A recent infusion of capital covered a new engine head, an air conditioner evaporator, window tinting, and a paint job—all of this, rather than incur the long-term debt of a car loan. Tony avoided long-term debt like the plague. Hell, with all these enhancements, the Blue Bolt should reach 350,000 miles. Beneath the comforting shade and rippling branches, Connie was kissed awake. Sleeping Beauty stirred, stretched, and stared straight ahead.

"That was a deep sleep. What time is it? Did I say anything that could be used against me in a court of law?"

"It's twelve minutes after eight. Too bad, 'cause we made it in rally-winning time. Oh, and your slumber-induced secrets are safe with me. I'll unload and get the bags to the room. Then I'm going to change and take a quick swim. I have some work to wrap up before the real fun begins. Did I tell you that you are beautiful today?"

"Not since we left the apartment. Thank you for the words and the incredible last night. Four times, very nice."

"No wonder I'm tired."

Only two small bags—Tony's canvas gym bag and Connie's leather tote. Very few clean clothes and some replacement toilet articles in each bag. Most of what was needed for attire and beauty maintenance stayed at the shore. Reason: less lugging. In his bathing suit, Tony trotted purposefully to the shoreline and directly into the water. Never a hesitation. Through the surf to beyond the sandbar, he dove into a wave. The invigoration of the water temperature, saline content, and currents left him gasping for breath. A few dozen deep hard strokes out and back loosened the remainder of the week's pent-up stress. Finally back on shore, Tony flopped on the large Big Apple beach towel, a remnant of Fire Island debauchery years. The sun began to warm and rejuvenate his body. One-half hour and he returned to the house to complete his report. Bill had not yet arrived.

Tony changed into baggie shorts and a T-shirt. He went commando, grabbed the laptop, and headed for the sunroom to work, entering the NYPD files. As of ten a.m. Saturday, Bill had not been questioned or arrested. Obviously, he had not reported Charlotte missing. Odd. He surely went to her apartment. If so, he had seen the crime scene tape. He would call the precinct. Not to worry, yet.

Downloaded all the files to complete the report. Reviewed the on-scene reports with the partial summary of last night. Dr. Cut Up's blood and chemical analysis indicated substantial levels of cocaine, marijuana, amphetamines, and barbiturates in Charlotte's system. There was GHB, the date rape drug. Did the *perp* use that to subdue her, before he went through the ritualistic event? She was a mobile pharmacy. Now immobile. Noticeable liver damage due to drinking and drugs. Lungs reflect heavy smoking. Analysis of all internal organs suggests a woman ten to fifteen years Charlotte's senior. No vaginal penetration. Traces of semen on knee only. And the sperm is damaged. No contusions or abrasions except where the tape had been applied: the mouth, neck, wrists, and ankles. Fetus was male, about ten weeks old. DNA tests on semen, fetus, blood, and cigarette would answer a lot of questions. Nothing really to add to the form. He completed CAT 1221. Loaded in the exchange files for the investigators. Tony also copied the file on a personal disc for CYA. Locked the disc in a box behind the suitcases in the closet. He sent bogus memos to himself as the last message online. He had to be sure there was no trace of communication. Disconnected. The process had taken two uninterrupted hours. To lunch and then back to the beach.

Connie awaited him on the deck. Scraps of breakfast, a partially filled coffee mug and the *Times* were before her. She was resting her eyes as the sun heated her world. Obviously, nothing in the paper about the murder. Towels and small cooler in hand, they headed to the beach. The sand got so damned hot it could sear feet while the sun was broiling the rest of the body.

"Has anybody heard from Bill and Charlotte? There was no message on the machine from them last night."

Connie seemed to be addressing the general populace.

"Bill called me Wednesday and told me he had to go to Boston for a Friday-Saturday conference of managers," Red responded. "He will be back in the city late Sunday. Did not hear from Charlotte." Red Saylor was the central clearinghouse for all communications. He had the staff and electronic equipment to relay messages to all from one or to one from all.

"That leaves Charlotte among the missing. I'll bet she went with Bill to Boston. Ya' know a little get-away for the loving couple. They have been very close and secretive of late. It wouldn't surprise me if they were to make it official soon." Mildred sometimes acted as if she were everyone's maiden aunt. A cup of personal half-knowledge mixed with a dash of innuendo was her favorite recipe for conversation.

"That leaves the six of us to fend for ourselves. Can we do it, team?" Dan asked, ever the booster.

"Who won the rally?" Babs always wanted to be in the game.

"No one was even close. Traffic is the great equalizer. Big pot next week." Red always knew the score.

"Shall we cook in or lay waste to a fine restaurant like the Shanty. I don't mind being in charge of shopping and preparation. But, I'll leave it to a vote. A show of hands to keep me in the kitchen. Okay, that's two. A show of hands to destroy the Shanty. That's four. The Shanty wins and losses. I'll make the reservations for nine. That should give us ample time to become radiantly beautiful and have numerous adult beverages. Now, since I have done the tough job, who wants to food shop for breakfast and luncheon items?"

"That's great, Tony, The Shanty it is. We picked up some snack junk food for horsies doo-vers. The rest we can forage for on Sunday."

Babs, the nosher, had spoken.

"The tough decisions are out of the way. Who can catch me?" Tony took off at a trot. The heat of the sand accelerated his pace. Connie, Red, and Dan joined in the chase to the waves. Kids always love the beach. After the beach san comes the rinse cycle.

As Tony was undressing to shower, he peeked at his pager. The numbers, three-six-two-four-five told him that he had email. The message was obviously from the precinct. He booted, entered the shared files, and opened the urgent message from Dr. Cut Up.

Victim and the fetus were HIV-positive. Trace of GHB found in initial screen leads me to believe she was drugged, but aware of everything that was happening. Unable to fight her attacker. Rather like suspended animation. Guys who use the date-rape drug like to see the fear and helplessness in the eyes of their victims. There I go, sounding like a shrink again.

The second message concerned Bill Davis. It was downloaded from the wire service and forwarded by Captain James Brainerd. Brainerd was the only one on the force who knew Tony's friends outside the force. The captain was Tony's Dutch uncle.

Taunton, Mass. Approximately two a.m. Saturday, Mr. William T. Davis of New York City died of multiple head and body injuries as the result of a single car crash on old US Highway 1. Mr. Davis's rental car apparently went out of control, left the road, and crashed into a concrete wall embankment. Initial police reports state that there were no skid marks on the highway. The car was engulfed in flames, which were extinguished by the Taunton FD. Rental records provided the victim's name and home address. Mr. Davis was the only passenger in the car at the time of the crash.

Captain Brainerd knew that Tony would want to know about Bill Davis. With those two messages, those two pieces of information, Tony had become enmeshed in the murder and death way more than he wanted. Information like this would make him more than just a gatherer and spectator. How hard was Uncle Jimmy pushing Tony to be more deeply involved? Unfortunately, the two emails explained nothing, yet hinted at everything.

Charlotte was infected. Did she give the disease to Bill or he to her? In either case, she was infected and pregnant. They quarrel, and he kills her. How did he know how to kill in that manner? If he used the date rape drug, he must have been incredibly pissed off. He wanted to see her suffer, knowing she was being watched. He goes to Boston and kills himself out of remorse or anger about the disease, the baby, or both. The question now is how much should I tell the denizens of The Bluffs?

The rich yellows and oranges of the sun interweave with the deep blue and purple of the evening sky and the puffs of clouds brought in by the afternoon sea breeze. Intricate plaids using all the colors of the spectrum confirmed that God was a Scot. The heat of the day was being supplanted by the cool of the evening. Six adults had taken their usual seats on the porch, drinks in hand, eyes staring into the fast departing day. Just like a friend, who was leaving. Tony had to tell them.

"Folks, I have some very sad news. I have learned that both Charlotte and Bill are dead."

The gasps and questions were all pervasive like Phil Specter's wall of noise.

"How is that possible?"

"What the hell happened?"

"Did they die together? In an accident?"

"C'mon, you're joking. And, it's not a nice joke about that sort of thing."

"Before we get too far, let me give you the details that I can. Please understand my position as both a friend and a member of the NYPD makes this very difficult. Charlotte was apparently murdered in her apartment sometime between noon on Thursday and early morning Friday. I can't give you more details than that because the murder is under investigation. Bill died in an auto accident outside of Boston. Both sets of parents have been notified. It will be up to them to make funeral arrangements. That's all I know as of now."

The silence was deafening. The stillness was overpowering. It even masked the surf.

"Well, I propose a toast to Bill and Charlotte. May their souls reunite in heaven."

Red always knew a right thing to say. Babs was sobbing. Her body was trembling on the love seat. Connie was stone silent. Mildred and Dan were hugging.

"Is there anything we can do? Or, should do?" whispered Mildred, the organizer.

"We can have a night in their honor, a night they would have enjoyed. Great food, *waaay* too much to drink, and some loud and cheesy rock 'n roll music at Bilgewater. We should even expand our reservations to include them and leave two seats unoccupied in their memory. You know, like the Jews do for one of their holidays. Since we can't do anything to help them or undo what has been done, let's remember them as we knew them."

Dan, the gentile, was ever positive. "Let's lift our cups one more time before I call the Shanty."

The sweetness of Balvenie was tainted by the bitterness of loss.

The meal dragged on seemingly for hours. Rounds of drinks, numerous courses, and toasts that covered the lives of the recently deceased. The six adults staggered to three cars and headed cautiously to Bilgewater for some late-night rock 'n roll. Local cops were very understanding of the residents of the 215 houses in Mantoloking. Drunks and drunk drivers, if they were residents, had been tolerated since before World War II. Outsiders were not tolerated, drunk or sober. Bilgewater was a near-perfect saloon for the beach town. The beer was cold, the music was loud and bad, the place smelled like stale booze, and the bathrooms were dirty. The place served booze to those of real or proven legal age. The assembled throng was there for a very raucous time. And, they got it. The uniform of the day consisted of shorts, pullover shirts, and topsiders if you lived in Mantoloking during the summer or jeans, a T-shirt, and sneakers if you worked there in the summer. The best colleges and business schools on the East Coast mingled with the lowest quintile of the local high school classes. Saturday night was get-trashed night. The locals didn't seem to resent the intrusion of the gentry. At last call, the six slid to their cars for the two-mile, ten-minute drive home. Crashed into bed at three a.m., having wished Bill and Charlotte the very best.

There were no more questions on Sunday. Souls and minds had been purged by alcohol. The luster was gone from the weekend. The trip home was torturous.

Monday was looking good.

Tony got an email from the captain.

Tony, could you come and see me as soon as possible?

Captain Brainerd's written wish was Tony's command.

"Sir, what can I do for you?"

"Close the dar, will ya, me bie."

Brainerd's phony brogue meant the same every time. Tony's uncle wanted a favor that was outside the rules and regulations of the force. Avuncular manipulation.

"What do ya know 'bout Detective Elija Washington?"

"Good worker. Very thorough. Not particularly innovative. Well liked. Made grade about a year before me."

"What else, me bie? Anything not in his personel file? Do ye know any rumors?"

"No, sir. Well, there was some talk that he got his promotion because of his color. But that's just old-timer Irish jealousy."

"Well, I've been informed that he may have some problems. Ya know, of a very personal nature. And, I'd like you to do some of yer famous fact gatherin' and analysis far me. Could ya do that for yer captain and be very discreet 'bout it? I need to know before the IAB roaches come to me."

"You know I'll do whatever I can. But it would be helpful if you could tell me what I'm looking for, sir."

Deference always worked with Uncle Jimmy's ego.

"I don't know exactly, laddy. There are just some ugly rumors that I want to either bury or expose to the light of official scrutiny. Now, be a good detective and detect. I'm sure you'll find somethin'."

The last words stuck—*you'll find somethin'.*

What the fuck was that? Jimmy must know already what it was Tony would find. Why couldn't he find it himself? Why Elija? Why Tony? He had enough on his plate. Uncle Jimmy had to be thinking that Tony would do anything to bury a rival. Where to start? Not at the precinct. This issue had gotten to be personal.

Get Elija's home address and telephone number, as well as the expected stuff from the department's files. Residence at 160 West 18th Street. Wife: Chakika. Son: Nelson. High School: Regis Prep, College: St. John's, Class of 'eighty-four.

The rest related to the force: entry date, promotion dates, precincts, superiors, honors, blah, blah. *Communicate with Regis and St. John's. Official emails for information. The cover is that the force is updating files of key people and wants to confirm what we have. Both responses came back in less than two hours.*

The Regis file indicated that Elija was the only child of two doctors, who produced their child late in life. Living in Plandome, all three must have commuted to Manhattan.

Graduated ninth in a class of sixty-three. Math and science were his strengths. Led the soccer team to the city prep championships. Was appointed to the National Honor Society as a junior. GPA of three-point-eighty-five for four years and a 1340 SAT score. Full scholarship to St. Johns.

In college, he majored in Poli-Sci with a three-point-two-five GPA. Member of varsity soccer team. Joined debate team as a junior. Member NAACP. Detained by campus police twice for civil disobedience: MLK march two years running. Parents died in a plane crash coming home from vacation in the Caribbean.

Sparse to say the least. Too sparse? What about Elija's wife, Chakika Stowe?

This would be more difficult. The Bureau of Records and Licenses would have files on their lives. *Check marriage, birth, real estate, etc. etc. Call Pietro Alietti, a long-time bureaucrat and second cousin. He is a guide through the morass known as The Bureau. Uncle Petie will have the goods by this evening. Check shared files around eight.*

"Tony, this is Red Saylor. Can you talk now?"

"What a surprise. Sure, I can talk. And we don't tap the phones."

"That's good. Listen, I was wondering if we could meet for drinks this evening. I have to be downtown, and I'd like to talk to someone without making it official. Is that okay?"

"Sure. Where and when?"

"You know the McAn's on East Fourth? Could you be there around five-thirty?"

"See you there, Red."

This was weird.

The McAn chain of saloons was noted for its cheap whiskey, stench and greasy meat sandwiches. Two shots for four dollars was a standard "special." The patrons were the neighborhood locals. Bar stools and booths. Regular seats for regulars. No waiters. After adjusting to the smell and the air, Tony spotted Red in a booth. Drink started.

"Thanks for being here on such short notice, Tony."

Red was sweating, but the half-empty glass was not. Granted, it was hot outside, but even McAn has AC.

"Let me be direct. Tony, what do you know about Charlotte's murder?"

"I can tell you only what I read in the *Post* and *News*. Not much, I guess. Why?"

"Well, I have fed friends from my past. Recently, we were talking about stuff past and present, and they mentioned that Charlotte's murder looked suspiciously like a contract killing. One of them remembered a local case involving some guy who used an ice pick like the weapon that killed Charlotte. The fed didn't remember where or when the other murder occurred but allowed that there was little publicity. Do you think it could be the same guy?"

"I don't know. But there are three big logic gaps on the path of a Mafia hit. Number one: mob hitters spend a great deal of time in jail. Number two: If not in jail, they are ancient when they get out. So, they are too old to pick up where they left off. Number three: What earthly connection would a hitter have with Charlotte? I think it was someone she knew. The papers reported there was no sign of a struggle and that her body was loaded with booze. So, Red, I don't think it was the fed's alleged hitter. I think the men in black are yanking your chain. And what does it matter to you anyway?"

"Nothing really. Just curiosity"

"Bullshit. Pardon my bluntness. But you appear to be near trembling with fear. What do you know or what are you trying to hide?"

"Okay. But this is from a confidential informant. A name and persona you can't reveal. Years ago, before I went to work for my father's firm, I used my mother's maiden name and lived in Phoenix. I hated my dad and all his wealthy old-school pals. I was involved with people in some very lucrative and equally shady deals. The feds climbed all over us like ants at a picnic. I rolled and went into the witness protection plan. Came back east, was allowed to go to law school, and took my dad's name. I remember one of the big guys told me he knew muscle who used an ice pick. Normally stuck the target in the neck and let the poor bastard stagger around and suffer to death, like a bull at a bullfight. The feds are trying to scare me. Maybe squeeze me for something. I don't know why they told me what they did, except that— Okay, now I'm scared. I'm also very clean in my new life."

"And what were you expecting to get from me?"

"I need you to dig around and find out where the hitter and his former boss are, and if I am in real and present danger. If I am, I have one course of action. If not, I have another."

"There's not much I can do except go through normal channels. Otherwise, the suspicion meter registers a ten on a scale of one-to-five."

"I have a sort of scrapbook of information about the situation I mentioned in Phoenix. Here, read all about it. It's a place for you to start. Now I have to go. See you this weekend. Good luck in the race."

The nine-by-twelve-inch manila envelope bulged. Red was up from the booth and gone like a will 'o the wisp. Tony decided to open the history trove at home. Twice in one day, he had been asked to dig into someone's life past or present. The brass frowned upon efforts outside of official investigations unless initiated by the brass, but one excavation was for his uncle and the other he could sneak under the radar of precinct politics.

Tony's instincts and CAT training were exploding.

Are these connected omens or just serendipitous events? Is this the slippery slope at the abyss of ruin? His lifestyle had been very objective. Until today. All his safety has been dashed. Should he extricate now? Press on? Stop and hope everything will go away like a bad dream. No. Press on. Keep all senses on maximum alert. Trust no one. Be wary of help and advice. Pray for guidance.

At home, Connie's message to him revealed she would be home by nine. The Seven Sisters were working on the list of information to gather, who would be responsible for what, and when it would be ready. Time was now free to dig into the extracurricular investigations. Check shared files for Petie's message and files. Sure enough. Good as gold, the goods were delivered. Usual financial stuff. Elija's wife, Chakika, brought a child to the marriage. Byron Wednon. Her maiden name was Martin. She took Stowe as her name before she married Elija. Too many names. Was she avoiding something or someone? No mention of the boy's father. Note to ask Petie to check that tomorrow. Own their coop outright. That's good. Paid off the $600K in ten years. How was that possible? Who gave them a loan that big on their limited incomes? Did they hit the lottery or just live under the subsistence level for a decade? City tax records revealed joint income of nearly $200K last year. Tony knew Elija's salary. His wife must be pulling down the big bucks. What does she do? Before the marriage, she was making about forty K as a "business consultant." Must have done really well in the past years. Note to contact the bank and pull account records for years prior and years after the mortgage pay off.

Only flag was the mortgage. No criminal activity. No cars. Nothing spectacular, and maybe that's spectacular in itself. No one is that bland. Fuck it; skip Red's case. *Read Red's file tomorrow at the precinct. Make copies of whatever is deemed interesting. Go to bed. Run in the morning.* Pre-dawn Central Park was an important part of Tony's world.

CHAPTER 3

Twenty-First Precinct:

A rriving at six a.m., Tony left a voicemail for Captain Brainerd. Tony had researched Washington's schools and all city records and found nothing of an unsavory nature. Now what?

Brainerd hated voicemail. Preferred little notes. Everyone knew when someone received a Brainerd note, a bright yellow sticky on the telephone. After leaving his message, Tony checked his mail and phone messages. Computer told him he had mail from Dr. Cut Up.

DNA from the semen left on Charlotte Jenks and DNA of the baby in her womb are not, repeat not, a match. Plus, the DNA on the cigarette is no match for semen, Jenks, or baby. Four DNAs. Thought you would like to know.

Why does the good butcher think Tony should care? This should be part of her report, referenced in his. But he does care. How does he get Davis's DNA? He's buried. Or, is he?

Tony places a call to the Taunton police and learns that the remains of his beach buddy are in the Commonwealth of Massachusetts State Police Morgue. Another call confirms the present yet temporary resting-place of William T. Davis. And, yes, they would send a snippet of hair and a piece of skin to the NYPD Morgue for DNA processing. To arrive tomorrow. Better give Dr. Cut Up a heads up via email.

The day watch oozes in. The detectives assigned to investigate Charlotte's death have not asked Tony for any help or additional input. So, fuck 'em. Open the manila envelope from Red. It seems that Ray Edmonton was arrested on money laundering, fraud, conspiracy, and bribery charges. *A task force comprised of Phoenix Police, Arizona State Troopers, and federal agents raided the offices of...*

The nasty little details of a former life. How a worm was hooked and used for bait. How he wiggled off the hook. Gave up everybody and everything: lost his cars, house, boat, and all the money. Old picture of Raymond with a Little League baseball team. *Who was his kid? Where is his wife? Trial must have been fast and furious. The list of the busted seems to have been lifted from the Rome telephone book. Except the dirty city officials. Prison terms range from sixteen to twenty-five years.*

Raymond got twenty—obviously, nothing ever

served. Seemed the top man was Guido di Bretta. Easy enough to cross-check through the prison system. Still serving time in North Dakota. Just Indian reservations and federal prisons. Talk about being isolated from society. Tony had to check the Federal Crime Bureau Criminal Composite and Cross Match file. This gave details for all the bad guys who were still alive. Importantly, it also provided links between the bad guys and the various families. Particularly interesting to see the cross-continental and the inter-denominational connections. Guido's family composite is typically ugly. No hitters or pure muscle in the group according to the bios. Nada. Zip. Zilch. Zed. The Feds lied to Red. Why? What do they really want? Call Red tomorrow. Make him wait and stew a bit. Nothing better than a little mind fucking a friend.

Tony spotted Brainerd waving for him to come into the big corner office.

"So, ya found nuttin'. That's no surprise. I tol' ya' the rumor I heard was of a personal nature. To confirm the validity of this rumor will require that you put our Mister Washington under surveillance. Yer actin' like a rookie. If ya want the promotion, you'll have to learn to be a real detective and dig deeper, work harder. Now be about yer work, laddy. Close the door on yer way out."

Tony mumbled under his breath. "I have to keep Elija under surveillance on my own time to get dirt on my competition. This is bullshit. Who is setting up whom? Jimmy claims to be helping me get the promotion, but I've known the political weasel long enough to know he is doing this for himself. But why exploit me?"

Let Connie know about my late night, just not the re-al reason.

He sat in an unmarked car waiting for Elija to leave places to go to others. Wait again until he goes to another spot. Then home to the precinct. Lights out at eleven. Home to Connie. She never asked where he had been or for what reason. Trust. Lovemaking was mechanical.

The telephone rang four times. It was Red in a full-fledged panic.

"What did you find out?"

"Christ, Red, it's five a.m. I was up late on real police business. I'll call you when I get to the House. Now go back to sleep or Babs, or whatever you do at this hour."

"Tell me you what you learned now. I'm scared. When I got home last night, the feds left a message on my secure office line. They are threatening me with innuendo. I need your help."

"Here you go Nervous Nellie. From what I was able to garner, you have nothing to worry about. You and your schmutzig former life are safe. For Christ's sake, go back to sleep. *Now.*"

Tony decided to stay away from the precinct for the day. He'd phone in with some excuse, go to the gun range, gym, and have a real restaurant lunch. He wanted to qualify with the new, bigger side arms: Glock twenty-five or thirty- six or the Raven forty-five. The snub-nosed thirty-two had been enough firepower for his non-violent work. Something told him he should be carrying heavier artillery. That to-be-seen force coming from the shadows warned him. Bad guys carried semi-automatics. So, he should carry a body stopper. Tony noticed a familiar name on the sign-in sheet, Margaret Myers—Magee. *Wonder what happened to her after the divorce. Billy had become violent. Coke does that. Was that two or three years ago?*

Only three other people on the range. The officer at the cage dispenses two grown-up pieces after the appropriate forms are completed. Ear cans in hand, Tony heads for alley number six. The explosions all around him are sporadic. *Try the forty-five first. Load the clip. Cans on the ears. Press the button and up pops the villain. Fire at will.* First explosion wrenched the gun to two o'clock. Firmer grip. Tighter shoulder. Second shot steadier, but still a pull. More shoulder strength. Three, four, five. Felt good. Six, seven, eight, nine. Checked target. Three in the head and four in the body. Big spread on the hits. Two misses. Needed better results to qualify. Needed much better results to stop the bad guy. The Glock twenty-five was lighter. Grip and strength were still important. But not as important as steadiness. After two passes at the target, Tony was spot on. Next step: sign-up for qualification on the Glock.

Three alleys to his right was Margaret. She had fired more than fifty rounds, in the time Tony fired thirty-five.

"Hey Magee, how ya' doin'?"

"Tony, nice to see you. Doin' okay. Over a ninety-percent kill. Not bad for a little girl. How you doin'?"

Her raven hair is barely shoulder length. Her smile could thaw the Polar Ice Cap. Black-brown eyes looked deep into his soul and had to have seen confusion and frustration. She never lets on. Freckles on her face, arms, and hands. Also on other, more personal, parts of her body. About five-feet-five-inches tall and one hundred twenty pounds. Fingers long and thin, but not delicate. Seems to be in perfect shape. At least as good as he remembered.

"Trying to get ready for forty-five or nine-millimeter qualification. I still need a lot more time at the range. Hope to qualify in a few weeks. I'm through here for the day. Next stop the gym. Burn off some of the over-indulgence in which I have indulged. Keep fit for the force. How about you, Magee?"

"Well, I was going to play hooky and do some shopping. But since I've just confessed to my sin, I guess penitence in the gym is my next stop, too."

"Great let's work out together and then have lunch. My treat."

"You're on."

The gym above the range was a universe away from the old barely lit barn containing heavy-bags, jump ropes, medicine balls, an ancient eclectic set of weights, a one-tenth mile track, and lots of mats on the walls and floors for hand-to-hand. Today's version was two levels. Weights and all types of machinery on the lower level, a par course fifth of a mile roadway, and a huge judo/self-defense room on the second level. Separate changing rooms with ten stall showers and numerous lockers for both men and women.

Every area was brightly lit. And telephones were

everywhere. No one could hide from the office here.

The pair rejoined on the par course. The oval had ups and downs, hurdles, and potholes. The path narrowed and widened to make a runner shift body weight and change course. All in all, a two-mile run was exhausting because the way varied so much. If a runner did not pay attention every step of the way, a spill was inevitable. The two old friends tried to establish a compatible pace. After three laps, the mutual rhythm had been set, and they began to talk in short phrases.

"Magee, what have you been up to. What's it been? Two years? Three?"

"Billy and I divorced. Working Vice out of the three-four. I understand that your CAT squad is getting noticed downtown. You and the cheerleader still an item?"

Her anger or jealousy was only slightly below the surface. Her words were well chosen and somewhat bitchy, the perfect ingredients to raise his anger.

"Sorry about you and Billy. I've known you for over thirty-five years, so I'm not surprised. I felt all along you were too good for him."

"How about you? Were you too good for me?"

They slowed the running pace and increased the conversational race.

"Let's stop right here. I don't want to open old wounds or pick at old scabs. Yours or mine. The pain will go deep into our hearts. I'm sorry we didn't work out. I had personal demons that were beating me up. You were a potential casualty of my war. I had to walk away. I didn't want to hurt you anymore. Hoped that after all these years you'd understand. Let's move on to happier subjects like starvation, ethnic cleansing, or child abuse."

"Sorry, Tony. I just had to let you know I was hurt and pissed then. But no longer. After the run, I need upper-body work. Will you spot for me? I'll spot for you."

A poke in the eye followed by a flirtatious invitation. Same old Magee. Lunch would be better. Broiled fish, dirty rice, and broccoli with lemon rinds. A nice bottle of Chardonnay.

"Did you catch the Handyman Murder investigation?"

"What would that be?"

"The duct tape and ice pick murder."

"Yeah, we were the hunters and gatherers. Why? What do you hear about the case?"

"Well, I hear she was covered in cum and blood. Probably two or three guys. Boyfriend died in Boston. No leads. What can you tell me?"

Tony and Magee had exchanged knowledge. Openness had been an important part of their personal relationship. A relationship that started long before the force, long before college, when virginity was an issue. As they went through life, the relationship truly had been on again, off again. The on-again part was very enjoyable, but it always led to an off again. When Tony felt sorry for Tony or was feeling like he was king of the world, he would find her. They would drink and snort their asses off and fuck for days. Go upstate or to the Hamptons. Real Bacchanals. Skip work just like they skipped school years before. They got too much, yet never enough. It had been that way for decades and could be that way again if they let themselves tread on that emotional oil slick.

They left the restaurant. He went north, she south. A brush with the past had not scarred them. But it scared him a little. He liked what he saw and felt comfortable being with her. An old comfort. Few pretenses. And no promises. But was it seductive to the old way? Work is the payment for fun.

First Bank of Long Island had been Elija's bank forever. It was his parent's bank before him. The bank, as all good banks do, understands the delicate nature of any NYPD internal investigation. The need to cooperate in the absence of subpoenas. The Assistant Vice President is quick to provide statements for Elija Washington's three accounts for the years in question. Of particular interest was the frequent large deposits made into the savings account, the partial dispersal to money market account and a large draft to the bank to buy-down a piece of the mortgage. The checks, which totaled $485,500, were issued by Road Developers of Brooklyn. Due to the size of the checks, the bank had kept photostats of them. The banking laws required it. Twenty-seven checks were made out to CM Enterprises and endorsed for deposit with a business stamp.

Tony, could not decipher the corporate signature. The memo notation was the same—consulting fee. The company name sounded vaguely familiar. Bingo! Road Developers was run by Sonny "The Gouger" Gentile. The big-time low-life, who had been staked-out, wire-tapped, followed, photographed, and otherwise legally watched during a two-year investigation into thug influence in the building of highways and bridges on Long Island. Rumor had it that the investigation lasted so long because each time something was turned up, it got buried in hierarchy channels or lost. Remove one block from the protective wall, and it was immediately replaced by two others. Who was digging and who was burying or replacing? After a while, no one seemed to care about the investigation. Except maybe Elija.

How did business checks get into a personal account? What is the connection? Save this until Monday. Clean up the desk and check the electronic connectors.

One email from Dr. Cut Up read: *DNA of William T. Davis is no, repeat, no match for any of the other DNAs at the scene. And he was high on meth and booze when he crashed—literally and figuratively. The five involved are Davis, the baby's father, the semen donor, the cigarette smoker, and the young woman. She was busy.*

As more was revealed, less was understood. Charlotte was pregnant by someone other than Bill. This someone was the spreader of the killer disease. Picture this: She tells Bill about her plight. He's crushed and leaves town. ODs on speed and booze. Kills himself accidentally on purpose. Who killed Charlotte? How many? Why? The baby? Business? *Leave it for the gumshoes. They have the same facts. Meet Connie at the launching pad. Will win the rally this weekend.*

The departure time was exactly 6:17:35, which meant they must arrive at The Bluffs no later than 7:39:35 to cop the cash. Dashing for dollars. Eight hundred to be exact. In descending order of importance were the decisions on which tunnel to take, how to get to the tunnel, and then how far to push the envelope of speed to make up the "lost" time. The latter was easy. Eighty-five to ninety would not get the attention of the New Jersey State Troopers on a Friday night of the beach season. It just required that all driving be done in the left lane of the Turnpike and Parkway. If a slow-poke got in front, flashing lights normally resulted in the obligatory lane change for the retardant. The toll booths could be a hassle. Mom and the kids always seemed to be looking for change after they had stopped at the booth. Once in a while Tony "tipped" the toll troll on the Turnpike or put a little something extra in the change slots just to keep from slowing down.

It was now post time. And they were off.

West on Ninety-Sixth Street to the West Side Highway. Head south to the Holland Tunnel. The first leg was easy. Enter the drive at the Marina. Snails congested the racecourse. Weaving in and out of lanes created a tapestry of vehicle and brake light motion, tire marks, and exhaust fumes. Accelerator. Brake. Accelerator. Brake. An auto Samba. Constantly searching for an opening to gain one car length. Keep one eye on the lane to the right, one on the lane to the left, and both on the car directly in front. The dammed potholes were pockmarks on the skin of the speedway. The cars serpentined around the pocks. Some of the holes were nearly nine inches deep. Hitting one of these would rip a tire and bend the rim. The tire change would result in a long, rally-losing delay. A rear-ender, even a love tap, and the stop for the obligatory insurance data exchange would also cost the rally. The closeness and precariousness of the conditions plus the stupidity of the other drivers made this part of the road race the worst. Despite the fact that the AC was on max, moisture appeared on Tony's forehead, upper lip, and underarms. All of the internal aggression not exorcised during his time with Magee was now oozing out of his pores. But the frustration of the drive could be a killer. Road rage was a distinct possibility, particularly when $800 and the ego pump of victory were at stake.

Connie calmly read some financial document. A stack of business reading was new weekend baggage for her. Her trust in Tony was reassuring. Her athletic training allowed her to move in synch with the car. She appeared unfazed by the sudden turns and stops. Was she so wrapped up in the subject at hand that she was oblivious to the external turmoil? Or had this slo-mo, imitation-grade le Mans become old hat? Regardless, Tony must concentrate on getting to the Holland Tunnel. The traffic stops. This week's roadway constipation appeared to be less than a mile. Time not bad so far. Three minutes behind schedule for this leg. The big delay was from here to the Jersey side of the tunnel.

The feeder lane was moving slower than the rotation of the earth. Was the Mazda actually losing ground? How the fuck did the DOT expect cars from a total of eight lanes from four different directions to meld and mesh into two tunnel lanes? Courtesy be damned. The yelping din of horns and the screeching of tires caused by lurch stopping and rabbit starting could be heard over the AC and Ninety-six ROCK, Home of the Classic Oldies. Connie was unfazed. Finally, the tunnel. Now the stop and start was in a darkened tube under millions of gallons of fetid Hudson River water. Never a comforting thought. Tony's claustrophobia seeped into his conscious. He knew that if he didn't get out of the tunnel soon, panic was only fifteen minutes away. Light at the end of the tunnel was the Promised Land—New Jersey.

One toll and two lights before a twelve-mile stretch of the on-ramp to the Turnpike. Now, twelve minutes behind schedule. Time to fly over the long Port Authority Bridge spanning the piers loaded with shipping containers and enough compact cars for everyone in Ames, Iowa. Toyota, Honda, Subaru, Mitsubishi, Hyundai, and Daewoo are amply represented on the tarmac acreage. The sun got in its last eye damage as Tony and Connie headed west for about five miles at eighty-five miles per hour. Turnpike Toll Ticket line moved quickly. People, anxious to get to their beach houses and get drunk, grabbed the computer tickets, tromped the accelerator, and entered the real racecourse from the pits. Sixty-five was the ante. With a wary eye for the radar bandits and the unmarked patrol cars, weekend pilots increased speed. The acceleration was gradual and in line with other drivers. No one wanted to be first and attract the State Troopers. No one wanted to be last in line. There existed some form of telepathy, which produced a fluidity of ever-increasing forward motion.

There evolved a lane designation by speed. Right-hand lane was for entering, exiting, and therefore the legal limit: sixty-five. Speed in the middle lane ranged from seventy to eighty-five. The left-hand lane was for the fearless, minimum speed was eighty-five. There was no maximum. It was only what the traffic and troopers would bear. The different caravans settled into their ruts. Occasionally, someone wanted to move ahead, change into a faster lane. This was done only by permission. Permission granted with the blinking of headlights and only if there were two full car lengths between the soon-to-be-divided carriers. God save the asshole who wanted to change two lanes or drift to a slower venue. People had been known to miss exits because no one would let them move to the right. Tough shit.

The trident wave thinned at the off-ramp to the Garden State Parkway. Tony left the Friday night specials, who were actually going somewhere other than the shore. The toll trolls were doing their best to maintain the frenetic pace established miles ago. Exact change was the key to a seamless entry. Never, never stop. The crush of vehicles already on the Parkway more than compensated for the brief thinning of the Turnpike herd. Here were met the Minions of Montclair, the Nabobs of Nutley, and the Clowns of Clifton, who had already staked out their respective lanes and settled into their lap speeds. The Turnpike Travelers were interlopers. To the swift went the prize, to the hesitant the tail end of the line. To meld into a phalanx moving at near warp speed took a keen eye, a lead foot, and a cold heart.

Easing into the fastest lane, the Blue Bolt roared to

the next tollbooth. Two booths before the exit to Mantoloking. Then back roads and alleys to The Bluffs. Each toll was treated the same. Lower the window and toss change into the basket as the car shot between the concrete islands. The change was rarely processed before the car exited. The blinking red light and bell ringing were trophies of a successful shoot through. Rumor had it that two cars were able to get through on one toll if they were bumper to bumper at sixty-five. But that was just a rumor. After the first toll, Tony was two minutes ahead of schedule. This cushion was needed just in case the drawbridge was raised for fishermen returning to the Mantoloking Yacht and Tennis Club.

The second toll was only a few miles ahead. The DOT was very clever. They determined where to place the tolls to derive maximum revenue. After the shoot through at this second toll, the Parkway condensed to two lanes and became a five-mile ribbon of taillights. Those headed for Atlantic City, Ocean City, Beach Haven and Cape May must endure this for hours more. *Six miles south on SR Forty-One, over the bridge, and through the little artsy-fartsy town, to The Bluffs, we go.* The bad news: the bridge is up, and arrival time is 7:46. The good news: this weekend, no one won the rally.

CHAPTER 4

43 Ocean Drive:

There is no sea breeze this morning. The humidity is presently ninety percent. This is a typical Jersey Summer Low. Be careful early in the day, the sun in a cloudless sky can sting your eyes and blister skin. You see, the rays are intensified by the moisture droplets in the air. But the hothouse haze will burn off by eleven, and the humidity will drop to an acceptable level. Accompanying the shift of barometric pressure will be the onset of moderating offshore air movement. All-in-all, a nice day will cover the shore from Seaside Heights to Beach Haven. Now to get your day really moving, here is Side one: Record one of The Benny Goodman Orchestra at Carnegie Hall. The big-band sound at its best from WDUN Eleven-Forty AM, The Dune."

Tony's enjoyed the visions of his father and older brothers sitting in the living room listening to music perfection that flowed from the Stromberg-Carlson. That impressive blonde box held a radio, a turntable, and a near-priceless collection of LPs. Being raised on a musical diet enriched by the big-band sound and jazz of the pre-war decade sensitized Tony to the vast difference between music and the syncopated nattering of each era thereafter.

"Sweetie, I want to run to the UpperDeck to pick up some bolts and wire for the cat. Is there anything you need while I'm out?" Tony, already into his baggie shorts, was pulling a ratty athletic T-shirt over his head.

"Just a small filet mignon and an advance of two million dollars. One million from the IPO."

Connie never opened her eyes. She turned away hoping to fend off the verbal intrusion into her dream queendom.

The streets were not yet jammed with Saturday arrivals. The UpperDeck was a typical trendy, very expensive shop attached to the Mantoloking Yacht and Tennis Club. The pier, winter storage, boat repair bays, tennis courts, lockers, snack bar and patio engulfed a large portion of the small downtown area. It was the hub of the summer, the place to meet and be seen. Liaisons started here were consummated on the motor launches and sailboats moored in the harbor; an encore at sea was optional. Tony's purchase was completed. Six eye-bolts with wing nuts and two lengths of rigging wire for a total of $185.46. Factory value…about six dollars.

This place makes enough in four months to fund the other eight. Tony mused. *Ah, the summer rich.*

The hunter and gather returned. Connie took Tony's arm warmly as he sat at the umbrella table on the deck. A quick breakfast before working on the Catamaran.

"Honey, is there something wrong? You seem pre-occupied? Is it Charlotte's death?"

"Nah. Nothing really. I'm out of the loop as it relates to Charlotte. I did my job of collection. She is in very capable hands now—two of New York's finest wrinkled suits and scuffed shoes. Lots of experience, and even more time on their hands. They'll find the bad guy very soon. It is in their best interest to close and close fast. There's just a lot of shit going down at the precinct. Polit-ical crap. Posturing about my squad. People jockeying for the position of power. This diverts me from my real job of turning the teen into a real adult. Each time I get a case, there are just too damned many people looking over my shoulder, second-guessing me, and suggesting the obvious as if they had the secret of The Rosette Stone. Mountains of paper bullshit. It's temporary, so, I'm cool with it."

"Talk about mountains of paper bullshit. The damned financial people want everything but our month-ly cycles. They hope to develop scenarios based on three sets of assumptions. Then they'll try to sell all of them at once. One will stick, and our futures will be ordained."

"After I rig the sail and replace the line bolts, it's down to the sea in the ship. Give me about thirty minutes. Care to join me on the cruise?"

"Love to. I'll pack the baby cooler."

Loading the boat, dragging it off the beach, and

pushing away from the shore are tiring. Getting past the cresting, crashing waves can be an adventure. By eleven the tide was going out, and the offshore breeze was mild. So, the outbound leg was comparatively easy. The two of them looked like refugees from a clown camp with zinc oxide on their noses, tips of their ears, foreheads and Tony's small bald spot, as well as on the tops of their shoulders. Sunblock fifteen was slathered over the rest of their exposed bodies. T-shirts had been knotted on the webbing. Now they wore just swim trunks. Connie had an incredible body, sleek and powerful—very sexy because power was sexy. And she was proud that men noticed. Tony suspected that she enjoyed manipulating men by influencing their primeval drives.

About a mile and a half out, the cat was responding well, cutting through the swells and skimming over the water. A few hundred yards more and they'd be on the glass plain. The locals gave this name to the section of the coastal water, about a mile square, due off the landmass. The water flowed on either side of the glass plain into and out of the inlets, which formed the island of Mantoloking. Kids werere not allowed to be out here because it was too far from land. Kids could sail all over the bay. For grownups, this was sort of a marine sandbox. Tony and Connie had been out here numerous times. Sailed for about an hour. Drank a few Rolling Rocks. Talked and shared as adults. This was their time. Connie opened the cooler and cracked a pair. This was a good routine.

"Have you thought of where you want us to be in

five years? I mean, given my recent good fortune, I don't plan to work much beyond that. How about you?"

Tony smirked. "C, are you telling me that you will want to stay at home, eat Bon-Bons, and watch daytime shock shows? The real question is do you have plans for our future?"

"I know we've talked around our future before. But we've always stopped short of final answers to tough questions. I love you, Tony. That's the bottom line. I want to be married and have a family. I want to do more than cohabitate. That's the acceptable term, right? I mean, there's got to be more to us than this. I hope that was not too blunt?"

"No. Not too blunt, sweetie Very straightforward. I realize I've been self-involved in the force and my advancement. And getting back from the abyss has not been as fast as I hoped. Perhaps, I haven't given our future enough time and attention. I am not ready to scale back on my ascent, and I like our relationship as it stands now. I know that whatever I do, I want to be with you. I care very deeply about you. These are good male-like instincts. I confess I have not considered children or anything more than co-habitation, but maybe I should. If I wait for all the right signs to make a commitment, I'll be an old man. I guess I'm saying I may be ready to take the next step. The big step. I'm sorry, does that sound like a wuss? I am attracted to the idea of living my life with you. But I'm scared because I'm not totally ready. I don't have control. I'm somewhat confused about my feelings."

"I understand. I understand the man and most, if not

all, of his baggage. I love you, too. So, I'll say it. We should start the wedding wheels in motion. It'll have to be after our IPO. How about next year at this time? Down here, at the shore."

"Okay, but let's keep it quiet for the summer. I couldn't deal with the fawning. Fetch me another beer, sweetie."

"You got it, Captain."

A sinking feeling crested over Tony and settled in his gut. Someone other than Tony had just made a life-changing decision about his life—a life-changing decision that he was not ready to make himself. Control had been ripped from him. The feeling resembled dread, like an unforeseen force was lurking in the shadows. Although he normally trusted his gut reactions and stopped before he spoke or acted, today it was too late. He could listen to the whisper of warning, but he could not rewind the tape. The die had been cast, the deal done.

Just as the first long tug was completed and the bottle secured in his caddie, Tony noticed that the small gray clouds had become large and black. They filled about a quarter of the sky. The weatherman lied, in accordance with Chamber of Commerce instructions. Or, this was a typical strong yet brief summer downpour. Getting caught in a squall, this far out, could be tricky. Time to race for home. Life jackets were strapped on both captain and crew, and the cat was pointed for the shoreline. Racing the storm caused adrenaline to rush in both of them. Truly masters of their own fates. Driven by the wind, the boat charged and crashed. Tony had to take numerous short jibes to reach the shore as quickly as possible. Connie jumped from side to side, leaning over the pontoons for balance as the cat lifted one leg then another in response to the gusts and the turns—tip-toeing across the water. Maneuvering through the roiling waves at shoreline was best done with all due dispatch. The sail was pulled down as the pontoons scraped the sand. Tony and Connie leaped from their perches, grabbed lines, and pulled the cat twenty feet up the beach. Exhausted, they plopped beside their water sleigh as the raindrops began to pelt the area.

"Not bad for a couple of lubbers."

"Connie, fear drives. Fear of death, fear of no control, and fear of disapproval. We were driven. We did well, sailor. Now how about we get smart enough to get out of the rain. Race you to the house."

Holding hands, they sprinted to dry space. As they entered the sunroom, they spied Red and Babs napping on separate couches. Tony and Connie stealthily headed upstairs to shower and change.

"Ladies first."

Connie sat on a small bench by the vanity and began to peel off her shirt.

"How about both of us first?"

Tony was removing his trunks. Then both of them stepped over the three-foot walls of a Grover Cleveland-size tub.

Tepid water to wash off the sand. They twirled, one at a time, into the shower stream. They gingerly swapped places, rubbed sensitive body parts, and exchanged kisses. Now to lather. This was why liquid body wash was invented. No loofahs, just two oversized cloths loaded with liquid soap. The rest of the sand and the residual of sunblock disappeared under the foam application and swirled down the large drain. The massaging took on another character. Soothing yet stimulating. Rubbing, but not kneading. Neither of them was in a hurry. Neither wanted to hurt. Face to face the other was bathed. Bodies pressed upon each other. Legs between legs. Groins pulsating with the hand motions and the water flow. Tony's back was rinsed. Connie's back was rinsed. Overall body stimulation. He dropped to his knee and started the purification of Connie's feet, legs, and torso.

The washcloth, followed by Tony's mouth, glided upward from shin to thigh to mons to belly to breast. The scents of sunblock, pectin and berries were enhanced by body warmth. The flavors, intermingled with the natural oils of her body, were enthralling. Up the right side and down the left. Re-contacting the entrance to the valley of life. Down the left thigh and shin to the foot. Scrubbing each toe, the ball, and heel. The back of each leg and the buttocks offered well-defined fields of flesh. Malleable. Spreading her cheeks allowed Tony to flow soapy water down and into Connie's hidden pleasure spot. Hidden to everyone but him.

Now, it was Connie's turn. Glassy-eyed, she kneeled before her god and discarded the cloth. Her hands were strong and well-motivated. Applying lubricating cleanser and creating a foamy medium of exploration, her voyage of pleasure was languorous. Tony's leg muscles were taut. She washed both legs. As she touched his shaft, it twitched with anticipation and his abs contract. Lather and rinse were followed by soft lips and hot mouth. Once, twice, thrice. Connie withdrew and moved up to Tony's chest where she nipped his nipples, all the while caressing his shank. Tony turned upon prompt. Her hands slid down the back of his ribs and separated his cheeks. Fingers entered the crevasse and gently probed his aperture. A pronounced twitch in front was the reaction. Connie stood. They completed their rinse and exited the huge antique tub. Towels were tossed on the bed as their foreplay drove them to complete the divine task at hand. They rested in an embrace and dropped into a deep sleep.

The rain lasted all day. When the lovers awoke, there was the chill in the air that always followed a storm. The sun was setting, and gaps in the lingering clouds created rays like so many odd-shaped laser beams from God. Time to brush hair and teeth, and put on fresh linens for the evening. Downstairs, Babs and Red were already sitting on the patio diligently working on their second round. Dan and Millie were in the bar and kitchen respectively. Prepping for the eve.

"Can I get you two anything to drink?"

"Yes, thanks. Two Balvenie. The usual way. Has anyone thought about dinner? Our nap sort of took us out of the real world for the whole afternoon. Is there anything we can do?"

"Connie, could you help me with the cheese and crackers?"

Tony took the two drinks and coasters to the patio.

"Well, if it isn't the upstairs nappers. I mean, we crashed before the storm and, I guess you guys crashed during. We got up only an hour before you. I guess all of us were exhausted. Where were you and Millie during the downpour?"

"We went out for a very late breakfast then some horrendous French film at the Bijou. Not enough T and A or implied perversion to bother. By the time the cinema ordeal was over, so was the storm. You should see the pools of water on the road. It took us about forty-five minutes to get home from downtown. I've walked the distance in half that. I'm famished. Where shall we go for dinner?"

The evening started with cute conversation, subsisted on chitchat, and ended with pleasantries. An evening of the banal. Tony had been aroused by the day's shower activity, and he wanted more. After two nightcaps, he and Connie headed upstairs. Before heated intimacy, there was interrogation. Quid pro quo of a confusing manner.

"Who do you think killed Charlotte? I mean if you can tell your future wife."

"Sweetie, I have no idea. There is such limited evidence, and much of it is conflicting. Why do you ask?"

"Just curious."

"Bull."

"Well, don't be so dense. She was a friend. We shared this house, for Christ's sake. And she was murdered in a very terrifying way. I've not been questioned by your counterparts. Have you kept them at bay? If so, why?"

"I'm out of the loop. It's in the hands of the regular detectives. Hell, I don't even know who has the case. It's none of my business. I did my job. I turned over the evidence, facts, conclusions, and assumptions on CAT. Now I wait for the next assignment. Case closed, from my standpoint."

A small lie never hurt anybody.

"Well, can you tell me your conclusions?"

"Sure, that I can do. But I must ask that you sit on this information. Consider this pillow talk. I don't think that Charlotte was murdered by Bill. I also don't think Bill knew a damned thing about the murder. Most likely he died accidentally. I have no idea why Charlotte was murdered or who might fit the MO. But my guess is that the murderer was a friend, a guy with whom Charlotte was quite close—physically close. And I think he was deranged, maybe a psycho. He used the date-rape drug, GHB. I assume that is one of the angles being pursued by the detectives. I also know she was HIV positive and pregnant. Again, by whom I know not."

Tell some conclusions, just not all.

Connie settled onto his side and initiated the luxurious process of late night love. Her kisses were tender. Her mouth and hand actions were familiar and comfortable.

They headed back to the city on Sunday night. Monday, after a full day of office drudgery and a light meal, sleep was instantaneous. Tuesday was different. Tony's email box was loaded. The usual bulletins about bad guys and announcements from the city, the force, and the union. Once these were read and deleted, he dug into the file on Road Developers and Sonny "The Gouger." Who else was involved? Who signed the checks? What is CM Enterprises? How did business checks get deposited into Elija's personal account? The file was substantial with numerous links to other files. After an hour of scrutiny, the answers gave themselves up. Elija was the lead investigative officer. He had a layer of the force, the FBI, and the state police helping him. If one considered looking over his shoulder and monitoring every step of his work to be helping. Everyone wanted Elija to succeed. They could not afford to have him fuck-up. It would look good for all interested parties if laurel wreaths could be placed on the head of an educated, dedicated black man. He would be beholden to all those who helped. But, if the investigation failed for legitimate reasons, the "boy" could take the fall. He just couldn't cut it. A no-risk situation for the powers that be.

In a review of the Road Developers corporate papers and corresponding banking papers, identities were revealed. The majority stockholder was Angela Benedetto, who just happened to be the daughter of Anthony "The Basher" a really big piece of mozzarella on Long Island. She was also the wife of Sonny "The Gouger." The president and front man for the company was Alphonse Mirtan, an upright citizen, who had emigrated from Jamaica. He was active in all forms of civic affairs. Married with two children: Alphonse Junior, a site supervisor, and

Carole. Alphonse the elder's signature on the legal documents matched the ones on the checks. So far so good. Why were his signed checks appearing in Elija's account? Was CM Enterprises run by Carole Mirtan? Who was Carole Mirtan? Further digging into the lives of the children revealed that Carole Mirtan, became Carol Martin, became Chakika Wednon, became Chakika Stowe, and finally Chakika Washington. So, Daddy, at the direction of the Benedetto family, wrote checks to his daughter, wife of the lead investigator, to confuse, slow down, or stop the investigation. The bank was involved because it was the lender for most of Road Developers' projects. Elija's mortgage was a point below competitive rates. The builders had four lines of credit with the institution at three points under competitive rates. Most of the notes were one hundred and eighty days in arrears at any time. With lots of late fees. No one at the bank seemed to care. And the public paid for it all via phony cost overruns.

The computer log showed that Elija entered the file after the investigation was officially closed. He entered only once. Arguably for no reprehensible reason. Just to look at a case on which he had spent two years. But the real reason could have been to insert facts and documents of incrimination that he had kept from others and, thereby, he secured protection. Did Elija withhold the facts of the case to give the appearance of a failed investigation? Once he was ordered to stop the snooping, Elija must have inserted his land mines. Logic dictated that there was no way in hell that this case would be reopened in his lifetime. But logic was not always a policeman's best friend. A hunch was. Perps did things that were illogical. Hunches sensed the illogic. If the case were ever reopened with these new facts, Elija would take the heat and most likely get dumped. His handlers would be crucified for closing a case with so much incriminating evidence. So many starts and stops. So many unanswered questions. The handlers would lose their pensions, and probably they would do hard time. Something no law enforcement officer wanted to do was be behind bars with the thugs he sent inside.

The appearance could be that they knew of Elija's nefarious deeds and wanted to protect their "boy," so they closed ranks and called it quits. Perhaps the higher-ups also were on the take and Elija knew about that. If the handlers were on the take, maybe they got to the bank to entrap Elija with the money. But so much money over so long a time eliminated that scenario. Were they also in bed with Benedetto? Was it possible that the bank, the feds, the force, and the mob were all naked under the sheets? All making money from state and federal road contracts? If this inconceivable were conceivable, Elija would be the fall guy and not the real villain. Although, he did take the money and was, therefore, guilty. So, if he rolled, he would get his wrists slapped. He would keep his life and stay out of jail. Whoever would be after him would consider him bait for the bigger fish. Much bigger headlines. Hell, he maybe could get a promotion. Stranger things had happened.

This delayed entry might be just the first page of his

insurance policy. Did he have more information in personal files? Information that would protect him against taking the fall for graft and a failed investigation that probably cost millions of dollars in personnel time.

Is Brainerd involved? How was he connected to the investigation? Or, does Brainerd want this investigation reopened to advance his own cause and raise Tony over Elija? Then Tony would be beholden to Brainerd. Did Brainerd know all along and want Tony to be the good guy to the public and bad guy to the brass? Is Brainerd taking heat from the brass that wants to sit on Elija and don't give a damn who else gets hurt? Who else knows about Elija's entries? No other entries after Elija's. Who knows what? Who has what? Tony decided to sit on the information for a few days. He needed time to discern the best course of action, how to get the goodies without getting got? The ringing reverberated through his musing.

"Detective Sattill, how may I help you?"

"God, Tony, you sound like you're doing take-out at the Fifty-Fourth Street Deli." Magee's tongue was as sharp as always. "Hey, I had a great time the other day. And I'd like to reciprocate the lunch part. How about today? I'll pick-up a picnic lunch from Zabars and meet you at the West Eighty-Sixth Street entrance to the park at twelve-thirty. See you there."

Tony had no chance to say no. He had no choice but to be there. Thank God, she was not dressed for work. A hooker's outfit would have been more than he could deal with. She wore a khaki skirt that came to just above the knees and a pullover sleeveless top.

Lunch was in a Zabar's bag as big as her smile.

No affectionate greeting, but she took his hand as they ambled to a shade-covered table for their repast. For her a turkey, cheese, bacon, and coleslaw combo on whole wheat. For him, very rare roast beef, extra sharp cheddar, and mustard on seeded rye. Chips. Two huge pickles. Seltzer at room temperature. She remembered everything.

"A picnic is fun. Listen, I had such great feelings after lunch the other day, I wanted to continue them for a little while longer. I was angry with you for the way you behaved years ago. But I understand that I am partially to blame for the break-up, and always responsible for my feelings. That was adult-sounding, wasn't it? I'm not sure where I see this re-meeting taking us, but I wanted to see if you feel as good about it as I do. It's okay. You can interrupt any time."

"Magee, I just don't know what to say. Yes, seeing you was terrific. Touching base with a very close friend is always good. And maybe we should continue to do the what-has-happened-since game. Maybe not. I don't know what my feelings are, or if I should have any, or if I should remain guarded. Yes, I am confused. And, since I don't want to say anything that could hurt you or be misconstrued, I think I'll just shut up."

"That's no way for a close friend to be, sullen and silent. Let's talk out the old feelings—kind and hurt, we can handle it. I know we can."

"Not now. Not here. Not yet."

"Okay. Where then? How about my place for a few

drinks after work Wednesday? No strings attached. I'm sure you can have an evening without the cheerleader. I'll bet she has them without you."

That was an odd dagger. Does Magee know something? Is she just fishing for a raw nerve?

"Of course, I can do whatever I want whenever I want with whomever I want. Do you still live on Bleeker? Good, I'll see you at six, unless something comes up. Now I've got to kick the dust off and head back to the ranch."

"Oh, you cowboys are all the same—work, work, work."

"See you Wednesday night."

The afternoon was filled with paperwork. Forms to summarize forms. Forms to advise. Forms to request. Then back to the range for more work with the artillery. Tony's hit rate was surprisingly better: forty-four out of fifty. Again, better with the Glock, even though he fired this first. The forty-five was just too damned heavy. *Go with the more precise destroyer. Sign-up for qualification as soon as there is a spot available in the class. Practice again next week.* At home, he checked his police force email and voicemail. Nothing of immediate importance. The ringing of the phone broke the silence of email reading. It was Dan Bren.

"Hey, Tony, Millie and I were thinking. Maybe we should have a real BBQ this weekend. It's something that Millie really likes to prepare. I'll work the pit Saturday. Wadda ya say, partner?"

"Who can resist such a generous offer? What can we do to help?"

"If you and Connie could do the salad and beverage, preferably lots of special beer. Babs and Red promised to do bread and dessert. It would be a big help. Millie and I were thinking this might be a healing event for the six of us."

"Sounds great, we would love to do our part."

"Okay, then, it's set. See you Friday night. And by-the-by, we kinda hoped you'd agree there should be no race this weekend."

Connie was very busy with the myriad minutia of the IPO. They hardly saw each other, except to pass in the bathroom or kitchen. When they were together, both were preoccupied. Wednesday after work, Tony took the all-too-familiar IRT number four local to the Village. Three blocks, two lefts, and he stood before her brownstone. The apartment was a gift from her parents, she owned it before Billy moved in and after he moved out, or was thrown out. Buzzed in, Tony climbed the three flights, knocked, and was allowed to enter.

"Hello, stranger, how was your day?"

"Well, ma'am, probably not unlike yours. Forms and paperwork, interrupted by inane telephone calls."

"Tony, you look terrific."

A pair of khakis and a pullover was neither special nor overdressed. He knew he looked tired. The pressure of the Washington investigation was beginning to show. But, Magee looked stunning. Jeans, a halter-top, and no shoes. Hair pulled back. Little onyx ear studs replicated her dark eyes. She had the look of a child-woman. She was a woman-child years ago.

"Magee, I've got to say you are *stunning*."

Her smile hinted of a conquer.

"Would you like a drink? I believe your favorite is Balvenie and spring water, tall glass, no ice. I'll pour two. Can you find the couch?"

The couch, where he had slept once too often, faced the fireplace in the front portion of the living room. Two huge windows looked out on to the street. The back of her apartment looked onto the backs of similar buildings and two backyards. He settled in for a pleasant evening with a dear friend. Something felt just a skoosh off kilter. Not a dread, but a feeling.

CHAPTER 5

160 West 18th Street:

Tony's turn to head another CAT squad. The site was downtown. The same MO. Woman nude. Stabbed once in the neck with what appears to be an ice pick. Taped to the wall in a crucifixion motif. Blood caked on the body. Dried goo on the knee. Looked like semen. Cigarette butt on the floor. Different brand than before. This one was a Vantage. No murder weapon on the premises. No sign of a struggle. No overturned furniture or visible stress. Was this the same perp or a copycat? How were the vics connected? Body cold, found by the housekeeper. The victim was Chakika Washington. The late Mrs. Washington has been dead probably twelve-to-twenty-four hours. Where were her husband and child during this time?

Tony was in overdrive. "Please be sure this gets to the ME's house for an immediate autopsy. Tell whoever works on the *stiffette* that Dr. Cut Up worked up the last one and to check the doctor's files. This looks too spot-on to be a copycat. Certain things like the cigarette butt were not released to the press are here. I want DNAs on everything—semen, cigarette, vic, and fingernails. This guy is too ballsy for his own good. I don't like being slapped in the face. And for sure the brass downtown doesn't like this affront to its image of guardian. Download all files by seven. I'll have to work unitl tomorrow morning to get it ready for the masterminds. No one on the night shift is capable of handling this. The detectives who caught the first one will want to start bright and early on this very high-profile case. I'll let the brass know who the victim was. They'll have to find her husband and handle all the PR."

Captain Brainerd was notified. He advised the powers at One Police Plaza. He told Tony that Elija was with his son on some hiking trip in the Appalachians and could not be reached right away. This would give the detectives a brief head start.

Tony read the headlines. *Handyman Nails Another.*

The *Post* could never be accused of subtlety. The paper named the victim. Her connection to the force. The similarities to Charlotte's murder. No connection to Charlotte. No mention of semen. No cigarette butts. The usual comment from *an unidentified source in the New York Police Department.* The leaker leaked a few inaccuracies for obfuscation purposes.

Dr. Cut Up confirmed case similarities: death; roughly same amount of time between death and discovery; no struggle, probably because of the trace of date rape drug found in her system; meal from the day before in her stomach; and some alcohol in Chakika's system. No penetration. No oral sex. The multiple DNAs would not be ready for a day.

Is there a gang? Is this a group thing? Do people watch as the vic dies? Some kind of sex club?

The final report was turned over to the detectives and Charlotte's case was immediately promoted to the head of the class.

The push was on.

"Captain Brainerd. I'm still gathering information about Elija Washington. How should I handle the investigation in light of this recent tragedy?"

"Well, laddy, we don't know if he was involved in the murder, now do we? I mean, he could have set up the whole thing to happen while he was out of town. He could have ordered the hit to deflect any investigation into his past. He thinks, who would investigate a grieving widower? I'll bet Washington knew you were digging into his past. Could he be buying life insurance in the truest sense? Our boy Washington was with his stepson about a thousand miles from home, when he lost his loving wife. Pretty convenient? Ironclad, wouldn't you say?"

"So, what should I do about the investigation into his personal affairs?"

"Stay on him, laddy. If he's clean, tell me. If he's dirty, show me. Now go and do. The pressure from downtown won't go away just because the boy's in mourning."

Tony decides to sit on the investigation until he gets a better understanding of who did what to whom and why. He wants to stay at the precinct to complete his report. The information downloaded by the other members of CAT is all too familiar. Connie has to work late again. They plan to meet for dinner at nine at PJ Melons. Dinner is fine. They talk about Saturday. Connie will make the salad on Thursday evening. Tony will buy the beer then. Magee is on his mind. *What does she want? Can't mention this to Connie.*

The precinct in the morning was a madhouse. The two detectives assigned to cases were pouring over Charlotte's file as well as Chakika's. Lieutenants William Kelly and Michael Echlebaum. *Not from this precinct. Need to get their backgrounds.*

Kelly, about 45, had the personality of a Pit Bull with AIDS. Face of a Pit Bull, too. About five feet eight inches tall. Must weigh two hundred pounds. Little visible flab. Built like a linebacker. The demeanor of a prizefighter who should have retired six years ago. Lots of black hair—head, face, neck, and arms. He aggressively questioned everything. Took nothing for granted. To him, nothing was until he said it was. Crude mouth. He could humiliate an old salt. He had alienated just about everyone who ever had the misfortune to meet or work with him. He petrified perps. They feared he would bash them if their answers didn't satisfy him. They knew he had done it in the past.

To this Mutt, Michael Echlebaum was Jeff. He was about fifty, six feet three inches, and rail thin. Pointed face and wire-rimmed glasses. A pinky ring and black leather watch band. Very calm and almost diplomatic. Cerebral in his approach to the job and life. Spoke softly and formed complete sentences. Worst word out of his mouth was damn. Wore a blue double-breasted blazer, gray slacks, blue shirt, and rep tie. Mutt wore a pullover and khakis, probably had a sports jacket in the car. Without a doubt, it matched nothing. Mutt used a shoulder holster to show off his .50 caliber Desert Eagle cannon. Not regulation. He must have threatened the brass.

Jeff hid his piece in the back of his belt and, most likely, kept a small one on his right ankle. During an investigation, Echlebaum ran two or three theories at once in his head and the small notepad that he kept in his blazer pocket. Echlebaum let Kelly dig away at the dirt like a good doggie, then Jeff harvested the garden of facts.

"What more can you tell us about these two murders, Sattill?"

One of the ways old timers got under someone's skin was to mispronounce his or her name. In this case, Kelly chose to ignore or deprecate Tony's Italian heritage and call him, Sa-tile—the first rhyming with way, that latter rhyming with mile—rather than Sattill—the first rhyming with saw, the latter rhyming with teal. Tony would not fall for this gambit.

"The name is Sattill. Sounds like *Saw Teal*. And I don't know anything other than what's in the reports."

"Well, Saaawteel, you knew both victims, didn't you? Why ain't that in the reports?"

Did Brainerd tell him? "That information is not germane. I shared a summerhouse with the first victim, and I had met the second victim a few times over the years during police force functions. I knew her husband, and the three of us would spend time at the functions. We, the erudite, tried to avoid the rough and crude members of the force. You know the ones."

"You knew the first victim very well then, I gather."

"I saw her during the past few summers, never during the other months. Our paths did not cross in the fall, winter, and spring. She lived with a friend of mine who I didn't see other than during the summer. He died the same weekend she did." *How did that slip out?*

Both detectives made a note of the gaff.

"What's the connection between the two deaths?"

"Nothing, I think."

"Nicely answered, Tony."

Echlebaum was playing the good cop. He stared off onto some planet in the solar system *kreplach*.

"I'm sure you can understand our interest in the smallest details. We have a slightly opened window of opportunity to establish multiple theories and follow leads wherever they may take us until the theories either prove viable or dry and die. There may be something in your connection with two deceased. Not you directly, of course. But there may be something about which you and we are blind to for the present. An unforeseen factor or force."

"The files are open. I've searched my memory for any connection between the two victims but can conclude nothing. Besides, that's your job. I just gather facts for the investigative intelligentsia. I do a have a few unanswered questions of my own, which are not in the files. Who, in the sea of the local, state, and federal bureaucracies has ever seen an MO like this? How can the multiple DNAs be explained? What are clues and what are red herrings? Are these murders means or goals? Are we dealing with a serial killer who will just kill until he's caught? Or are we chasing a very clever executioner? I don't have the expertise of you two, so I'll stay out of it. If you need to talk to me, I'm here."

Tony had fallen into their well-honed trap. Bad cop pushes. Good cop pulls. A slip occurred, and information seeped. Tony had to see Brainerd and get some off-the-record skinny on these two. Had to be after lunch. The light was blinking. Magee. He didn't see her for years, and now she sought him out daily.

"Hello, handsome."

A dangerous start in a world where his phone may now be tapped, his every conversation monitored.

"I want you to know how wonderful our talk made me feel the other night. And, I want to see you again. Real soon. Like tonight. Come on by after your shift. We'll have a light dinner. Then you can go back to the cheerleader."

"Geez, Magee. Tonight is really bad. The investigation into the murder of Elija Washington's wife has me jammed up. The investigators are all over me like a bad smell in a small space. I'll have to take a rain check. How about next week? I'll call you on Monday. Okay? Have a great weekend."

Tony hung up before Magee could verbally protest. The flame was tempting the moth for a return visit. Not good.

Thursday evening was prep night for the weekend. Connie was queen of the salad. She could make an entire meal of different colors, textures, chews, fragrances, temperatures, and flavors. She also knew a secret dressing recipe and the exact amount that would enhance her creation.

For Tony, it was easy. Rolling Rock and Yuengling were the only beers. Only one store on the Upper East Side of Manhattan sold them both. The last of the D'Agastinos. The managers knew Tony. He could phone in his order. The cases would be kept in the meat cooler until he arrived on Friday. Then the two cases would be wrapped in pre-moistened and frozen newspaper, and then bubble paper to keep them cold and safe during the run to the fun. Any significant increase in temperature could damage the multi-layered flavors.

The price for this luxury was steep but worth it because it showed. In real life, form should follow function. But in the case of beer and all other visible aspects of conspicuous consumption function followed form. Accolades were accorded the individual who proffered the best-wrapped gift, or in this case, the most unique system of cooling. Who cared if it worked as long as it looked better than anything else like it?

Friday was here with all its childish hype. The drive to The Bluffs was quiet. Connie was not reading. She was brooding.

"What's wrong, sweetie?"

"Nothin' really, dear."

She never used an affectionate pronoun. Also, Tony knew that when a woman said the "nothing is wrong," something terrible, nay dangerous, was about to be put on the table.

"Tony, you seem to be drifting away from me and us as I try to get closer. So I ask you, what's wrong?"

"Nothing between us, Connie. It's just this damned investigation. I can tell you this because who we are, but I'm concerned. I am convinced that Charlotte and Chaki-ka were killed by the same perpetrator. What the connec-tion between them is, I don't have the foggiest idea. Why they were killed is anybody's guess. I think it may have something to do with me. Somehow, I am a link between the two homicides. But I am not *the* link. So, I'm preoc-cupied looking for that something that may not even ex-ist. And if I find it, I may not know that I've found it. Or what it is I've found. I don't subscribe to pre-destination. I am a believer in free will. I am suspicious of happen-stance. There are reasons for everything. I just don't know them. And it's driving me to fucking distraction."

"Whew, that's great. I mean, it's sad that the case is eating you up. But I'm glad it has nothing to do with me. I mean, I haven't done anything to alienate you? Right?"

"No, Constance Angelica Wilhaus, it's nothing you've done. And I am sorry if I gave you that impression. I love you and would never hurt you. You and I have a future together. Hopefully, children in quick succession—two boys."

"Whoa, stud, give me a break. Let us start with two kids five years apart and then survey the horizon for critical signs like the ravages on my body and your age. For now, I'm going to nap, while you pilot the Blue Bolt. I have no work for the weekend. I plan to frolic all day and fuck you blind all night. Sound good?"

"Sounds frighteningly great."

The crisis of *amore* was avoided. Confrontation confronted or curtailed. The evening was as promised, and sleep was deep. Before five in the morning, Tony set up his laptop and started digging in the NYPD Personnel Files. William Terrance Kelly had a three-page bio, lots of awards, and was a few years away from a decent retirement. He also had six commendations for bravery and three with bullet wounds. Either this guy was incredibly brave or incredibly stupid. Not married now except to the force. So, he was very dangerous. He worked out of SIU—Special Investigations Unit—and reported only to and worked at the pleasure of the commanders at One Police Plaza. SIU ferreted out bad situations before they could become public problems. Well, before Internal Affairs had to saddle up. Before, the Shitty Indians, as the precinct populations called them, were used as shock troops to control the spread of an evil which could severely damage the Force and the reputation of the commanders. The select group of commanders, to whom the SIU reported, was anonymous, like a Star Council. This shadow group made decisions to guard, keep, and protect the NYPD. These goals were held above all else: the public, the beat cops, and even crusading politicians. SIU washed any dirty linen before the press and the public saw any schmutz.

Can anyone say Nazi propagandists?

Michael David Echlebaum, Jeff, was similar to Mutt, except he had one fewer bullet wound, was more cerebral, and was divorced. These two-of-the-hidden-agenda were not good. These two believed that the end of a clean police force justified any means. Who got hanged on the public gallows was of no concern, so long as it was not the Force in general. The two investigators didn't care. And, certainly, the commanders didn't care.

Where does Brainerd stand in all this shit? Up to his knees or just to the top of his shoe soles. Does he know the final chapter before it is written? He is a pawn, manipulated to be sacrificed tomorrow. What was he doing to or for Tony?

These two and the commanders were condensed persona. They had lost all extra personality traits which could make them human. They were so focused on and so involved in what they did that they had become the things they did. They had no humor, no empathy, and no sympathy. They were outsiders working on the inside with extraordinary force. In the world of war, they were snipers. In the NYPD, they were members of SIU.

Connie comes down the stairs looking for coffee and a roll. Tony closes his laptop. The day is as calm as the ocean. No sailing. Just frolicking in the waves and preparing everything for the big cook-out. The precious beer is removed from its store packaging and planted in two galvanized tubs. Ice beneath, around, and over the bottles. Then the two tubs are covered with the wet towels and encased in bubble wrap. This rite of near freezing assures the ideal temperature of the beer; between thirty-four and thirty-eight degrees. The entire process takes an hour. Hell, the ice chips alone cost twelve bucks. But show was more important than tell. The salad, ribs, and sourdough bread make for a glutton's delight. Beers before, during, and after the meal.

This is a Eucharist for the Burial of the Dead: Rite 1. No readings, just homilies and humorous stories. Some Old Testament, some New Testament. No priest. No Consecration. That would have to wait for the real funerals. Conversation about Charlotte and Bill was all in the past tense. No tears. It wass as if they were just visitors, people passing through the lives of the remaining six. Not touching anyone deeply. Fun while they were here, but gone on the long trip home. Hope they called when they got there.

Morning brought an alphanumeric page and another trip into the Police Computer. An email from Dr. Cut Up: *DNAs. Victim. Semen. Cigarette. Semen on both victims, Jenks and Washington, is a match. Not so with cigarettes. Now you, Kelly, and Echlebaum know everything I know.*

Why was the good doctor linking Tony to the SIU guys? She couldn't be part of the *ubermensch* power structure. While on the system, Tony began to reopen the Road Developer case. He needed to check two sets of facts: Who were the handlers? Who ordered the case closed? The details should be found by revisiting Elija's last entry. *Get the names of handlers and crosscheck them with present files.* Five names. One deceased. Two retired. Two worked out of One Police Plaza. One of the retirees moved to Tampa, Florida. No phone number. The other retiree had moved to the Upper Peninsula of Michigan. *That's the way to do it. Move far away. Need to find out more about the presently employed commanders, Wilson and Weaver.* They were the youngest of the department higher-ups involved in the case, and they were still at the trough of public pittance. They had the most to lose—careers, pensions, and maybe even give up their regular lives for lives in jail. The personnel files revealed that they had worked with SIU almost since its inception in the '80s. Their bios boasted about civic responsibility, training programs introduced, and continued educational opportunities opened. Very clean and revered. *Too clean. Both of them. Dig more on Monday.* The state and federal mopes involved in the case were just names. *Have to contact a cousin in Albany and then ask her how to get the skinny on the non-locals.* Wilson and Weaver's names were on the authorization to close the case. The dead state police captain name…Slotkin…was there as was Byers—state—alive but retired to Florida, and Rissi—federal—in The Upper Peninsula. *Hope these two are still alive.* What a strange coincidence it would be if all three were absent from this Earth now that Tony was reopening the case that was improperly closed. Coincidence? Yeah sure.

Tony was going to be busy. The trick for him would be to dig faster than it could be buried.

Email to meet with Kelly, et al., at eleven downtown in the eighth-floor conference room. Not an invitation, more like a demand.

First, Toney downloaded what he examined and put it all on his personal disc so he could review it at home on his secure laptop.

Call cousin, Marie Antonelli, reacquaint her with her downstate family, and ask her for the favors.

"Let me get this straight. You're asking me to go into the state police personnel files and extract bios and an address for Byers. Then I am to email this not quite public information to your home computer in The Big Apple. Second, I am to get you a name of a discreet contact in Washington who can and will do the same thing for you from the FBI files for Rissi. Well, I can do the first half of the job. But it will cost you. I haven't figured out what yet. Give me a few seconds. The second half: I can't do what you asked."

"Marie, I'll take whatever help you can give and then I'll try to get the FBI information the slow way, through official channels. This will probably raise red flags and get my ass handed to me. But if it's gotta be, it's gotta be."

"I never said I couldn't get the FBI files, I just said I couldn't do what you asked. I'll get the FBI files myself and email them to the same address. Just don't ask how I get the material. If I tell you, I'll have to swallow cyanide after I slit your neck. Sicilians do that sort of thing you know. I can have the files at your home sometime late this afternoon. Boy, is this gonna' cost ya'."

"Whatever it costs, it's worth every penny."

"We're not talkin' money, Tony sweetie, we're talking my fantasy. Are you prepared to take care of that?"

"What about Al?"

"The jamoke skipped with some bimbo from the DOT. But enough about the past, let's talk about my future."

"If you're talking' about what I think you're talking about, it is not kosher between cousins."

"We're second, or maybe even third cousins, and I'm not talkin' marriage or childbirth. I'm talkin' a nice week in Barbados next February when the Albany snow is up to my inner sanctum. I want to be warmed all over— inside and out. Hey, you haven't changed since the last reunion, three years ago. I mean, you're still handsome, straight, and single."

"Two-and-a-half for three, Maria. That's the good news. The bad news is that I live with and will marry next year a wonderful woman. And, if memory serves me, you, too, are a stunning woman. You should have no trouble attracting the right man or men. I mean, I felt some level of attraction when we danced at the party."

"Your present situation is your problem. Yes, I am attractive. And I too felt the warmth of bodily desires on the dance floor. But if you don't want the info, you don't have to make the deal. Hey, maybe by next February, your plans will have changed and a week in the sun with the beautiful and lonely Marie will be the tonic you need.

By the way, I'll attach a photo of me for you to ponder. I need your verbal sanction on the contract now. In this family, word is bond. Now, should I get to work on your project and my winter vacation?"

"You got a deal. Thanks for your help."

What the hell? A lot could change between now and then. Besides, if he didn't get the material, there would be no vacation at all.

The entrance to One Police Plaza was guarded by dogs, uniforms, four cameras, and two metal detectors. All stuff was removed from the visitor's pockets, placed in baskets, and returned at the reception desk after probing by two uniforms. The sergeant at the desk required identification, sign in, and the individual whom the visitor wished to see. Fort Knox might be more secure, but One Police Plaza housed more power. The elevator ride to the eighth floor was a time for three more cameras to scan interlopers. Every step of the way the camera data was sent to monitors in secret booths in the bowels of the building. George Orwell was alive and working in downtown Manhattan. A reception desk could be found behind two-inch-thick bulletproof glass on every floor.

Tony was buzzed into an antechamber. Was he being scanned? He announced himself and the name of his host. Tony was buzzed into the reception area, and the officer behind the desk detailed his next stop. The conference room was entered through a single door. The room was long and sterile. There were no obvious viewing apertures. No mirrors or glass on the walls. But there were too many ceiling sprinklers for the building code. Which ones were real? Which ones were camera lenses? Twelve chairs sat along the sides of the oak-topped table. There were mommy and daddy chairs at either end of the table. Tony sat and awaited his grilling *du jour.*

Kelly and Echlebaum entered within fifteen minutes, appropriately late to instill anxiety.

"Good morning Detective Sattill. Thanks for coming downtown on such short notice. We have a few things that need to be clarified. Before we begin, help yourself to some coffee, if you like."

They conveniently misstated the facts that they referenced when they demanded the meeting to put him off guard. Echlebaum pointed to a credenza, on top of which were a coffee thermos, Styrofoam cups, sugar, and whitener. Tony declined the invitation. He did not plan to stay that long.

Mutt started. "Okay, Mister Sattill, here's the bottom line. You knew both victims. Your pussy squad was called to both scenes. There was semen found on both victims. That's a very sick guy thing. It was the same semen on both. Now, we don't think you're involved, except coincidentally. But we're trying to rule out suspects at the same time we pursue others. So, we think it would be a big help to the investigation and in your best interest to let the police lab run a DNA analysis on you. Wadday say? Quick. Painless. Hell, you won't even have to jerk-off into a cup, unless you want to. Just give us some hair or a fingernail clipping. Nothin' too personal. And it clears you once and for all."

"If you check the files, the department has my DNA.

It's required of everyone on the force. I am sure you know that. So, why the bad bluff?"

Tony poked the paper tigers in their respective eyes. But they didn't blink. "Thanks for the invitation to my hanging, gentlemen," he said. "But I must respectfully decline. I know my rights, and I don't want them trampled, or me railroaded. I am curious about something. Once you found me guilty through lab-test magic, how were you going to explain the different cigarette butts, Charlotte's pregnancy, and my whereabouts during the crimes? I have alibis for the time of both events. So, if you have nothing else about which you wish to converse, I will be away."

"We had hoped you'd be more cooperative. We thought you'd want to do the right thing by the victims as well as the force. Let me be very frank. This storm could get very destructive right now, and you're near the eye. You could get sucked up into the vortex and deposited on a gurney with arm straps and syringes. As a member of the police force, you can be required to submit to another DNA test. Just to confirm the data."

Jeff can get tough.

"To you, I'm a suspect. To me and my attorney, I am a private citizen. Therefore, you best have more than empty bluffs to proceed with this lunacy. Live with the data in my files. My personal attorney, as well as the PBA attorney, advised me of my rights. I don't think you can get the agreement of the brass for your fishing expedition. So, I repeat, unless you have any different topics, I'm out of here."

Partially truthful, but they don't know which part.

"If you don't cooperate, we'll be all over you like oil on a pizza. *Capice*, boy?" Kelly pronounced the word *kaypiece*.

"Well, paint me green and call me a leprechaun, Kelly, you're a bigot. Who would have thunk it, you ugly Mick pig. Get the fuck out of my face, my way, and my life, or I'll have my attorney wrap your potato ass in so much paperwork, you won't see your dirty eye for two years. Ba-bye."

Tony was up from the chair, out the door, and past the reception desk in less than ten seconds. Kelly stalked him menacingly, but silently, the entire way to the elevator. Score one for the good guy. But the bad guys would be back. Tony doubted his home would be bugged and his phone tapped until tomorrow. It would all happen while he was at work. The rats would probably get onto his precinct computer and lock on to his link to the mainframe. No court order for this activity. Therefore, it wouldn't be admissible in court.

But they could use the information to threaten, cajole, and uncover leads to other things nefarious. Real or imagined. But, why? Why the bad bluff? They knew that he knew that they had nothing. They wanted him to do something to help their cause. He was a person of interest. Interesting.

Marie was on time with the goods.

Holy shit! This is Marie? She is better looking than my memory indicated. The entire bikini must have been made from a single drink coaster. What a shape. What a face. What opportunity did I miss during the last reunion? How old is she? Too late now. Isn't it?

Tony sent the files to the printer then onto his disk. *Have to put the disk and the pages in the accessible, safe, and secret place at The Bluffs. Keep the material on me until the weekend.* State police captain was dead of a heart attack. The other lived in a nursing home for Alzheimer's patients outside of Tampa. She'd be a lot of help.

The FBI agent lived on a farm with his wife. Address and telephone number. Dead end was an ironic term for Tony's investigation at this juncture. He phoned Special Agent Thomas Rissi and explained the purpose of the call. It turned out that Rissi knew Captain Brainerd. Rissi and Tony exchanged personal antidotes about Jimmy.

"Sir, I am inquiring about a closed case conducted by Detective Elija Washington into the business practices of Road Developers of Brooklyn, New York. You are listed as the member of the federal task force assigned to the investigation."

"Yes, I remember that case. What is it that you want to know?"

"Well, the case seemed to be going nowhere and was closed quite suddenly, as you may remember. I'm trying to determine the details of the decision to close. Who gave the order and on what basis was it given?"

"Well, Detective Sattill, I don't immediately recall that information. Could you give me a day to collect the facts? I have some old notes, which could jog my memory. Could you call me tomorrow, about this time?

Then we'll talk. Let me give you another number. And I suggest you call from a pay phone. Let's get the time right. Seven-thirty in the evening your time, which is also my time. We'll keep our conversation to a minimum. Talk to you then."

He was too calm. *This is getting curiouser and curiouser. The day delay is so that Rissi can talk to Brainerd. But why the second number and pay phone? Of what is he afraid?* Of what should Tony be afraid?

CHAPTER 6

16 East 96th Street:

Four-thirty a.m. The radio. The running gear. The littered pathways. Shower. Breakfast with the *Times*. Connie remains wrapped in the arms of Morpheus as Tony closes the door. Subway to work. This morning ritual is comforting in its familiarity yet exhilarating in its execution. The precinct is slowly filling with the shufflers—out and in. No telephone messages, but three emails all funeral announcements. Bill Davis will be interred in St. Petersburg, Florida tomorrow. A service for Charlotte Jenks will be held tomorrow at the First Presbyterian Church in Columbus, Ohio. The Police Department of the City of New York requests that Detective Anthony Sattill attend the "Celebration of Chakika Washington's Life" at the Mt. Nebo Evangelical Church, Bayside Queens at eleven a.m. this day. The request was not sent force-wide. Tony's requested attendance was directed specifically at him.

Why the personal touch? Who will be there? Who would be watching?

Three children had gone home. Nothing was worse than when a child died before the parents. There were great lamentations, gnashing of teeth, and beating of breasts. Two email regrets. Tony had to go to Queens.

Petie unearthed nothing of consequence about Chakika's—nee Carole—husband before Elija. Wednon had left town two years ago. Tony emailed Brainerd about his planned trip to the other borough. He went home to change into something appropriate for the occasion. Connie had gone to work. The subway ride to the church seemed to take forever. He walked eight blocks. Cars and limos of all sizes lined both sides of the street. The uniformed brass was out in full force, a solid show for their "boy." Men in black suits accompanied women in dark-colored floral dresses and large floppy straw hats. The little children did not fidget, fuss, or make noise. They had been warned. The church was jammed, the service orderly. The preacher offered a compelling sermon about the meaning of life and its many phases, including the one we called death. Homilies from her husband and father. The church population was mixed: blacks and whites, soldiers and civilians. Good guys and bad guys. The top and the lower echelons. SIU was observing who was there. Tony rode to the cemetery with a couple of guys he had known since the academy. The graveside service was very emotional. All of the feelings untouched in Church exploded at the burial. The reality had set in. Condolences were expressed to the family.

"Tony, I think we should talk." Elija's comment had the impact of an ice cube in Tony's crotch. But he had to hide his reaction, lest somebody was watching.

"Elija, how about Monday."

"Dinner at my place? See you at seven."

Tony arrived back at the precinct around two. There it was an email from Magee:

Can I see you again? Tonight, okay? My place at six.

He needed to determine how he felt, once and forever. He spent the rest of the day with paperwork. The telephone interfered with the fun forms.

"Detective Anthony Sattill, how may I help you?"

"Who am I talkin' to?"

"Sir, this is Detective Anthony Sattill. How may I help you?"

"I have some information about the Handyman Murders. What's it worth to ya'?"

"Well, sir, I don't have any authority to distribute funds for information. But I will talk to my superiors. They have the authority to pay for information if it proves valuable to our investigation."

Tony was frantically waving for someone, anyone, to pick up and listen to the call. Someone else to contact Kelly and Echlebaum. And a third party to get Captain Brainerd to Tony's desk. All the while, Tony had to remain calm on the phone.

"Sir, I see my captain nodding to me that we can release funds for the right information. If I could get a few facts, it would help substantiate our request for funds. Just some basic data."

"No. Here's the deal. I know the people involved in both murders. That kind of information is worth fifty grand. That's what I want. That's what you'll give me. I'll call back in a while and give you the details of the exchange—conversation for cash."

Click!

Lights were blinking on the phone set. Kelly, Echlebaum, and Brainerd. A three-way call was set so that Tony could be debriefed. Kelly wanted to know why Tony didn't stall so a trace could be established.

"The guy knew exactly what he was doing, almost as if he had been prepped. He was off the line in less than thirty seconds. Not enough time for a trace. We'll be ready for his return call," Tony told Brainerd.

Echlebaum and Brainerd agreed that the caller offered nothing to indicate he knew *Something of Value*. They wanted to go slow before dolling out any money. Tony's handlers were happy. Equipment for the trap and trace was set up in the squad room. The phone rang again.

"Detective Anthony Sattill, how may I help you?"

"Detective Sattill, this is Dick Wallace at the *Post*. Why are you refusing the help of a New York citizen in solving the Handyman Murders?"

"Mr. Wallace, I have no idea what you're talking about."

"I have it on good authority that a private citizen has

some critical information that he wishes to share with the police force. But you told him you were not interested."

"Did this private citizen happen to give you his name? Or tell you what he knows? Or anything that can be corroborated by sane people?"

"Detective, that is confidential information. He is protected because he's a source. He just called my office and told me that he knows the people involved in the murders and that he told you this. You blew him off. What do you have to say about that?"

"First of all, Mr. Wallace, or whatever your name is, I'm not even sure you are who you say you are. Or, that what you say happened really happened. Consequently, and speaking for the New York Police Department—no comment. But if you have any further information, please call Captain Brainerd at this precinct. Thank you and goodbye."

He called Brainerd, Kelly, and Echlebaum and told them about this second call. They agreed to do nothing in reaction. Just wait for *The Information Man*. Tony's underarms were sopping wet. He needed to hear a friendly voice. He called Connie and told her he had to work late. She was cool with that.

He rushed home. Showered. Retrieved his micro-recorder. Then he was back into the transit womb of New York to be reborn in Magee's familiar neighborhood. Forty-five minutes late. Cops understood tardiness and the flexibility of schedules. She answered the door dressed to kill Tony's resistance. She was in her street-walker uniform. Really short shorts, the ones that showed the bottom of the two bottom cheeks. A scooped neck halter-top two sizes too small revealed the bottom two-thirds of her rib cage as it flattened her breasts and agitated her nipples. No shoes. Hair pulled back to flash her ears, a weakness of Tony's. Magee was Daisy May to Tony's L'il Abner

"C'mon in, hunk. Make us drinks while I unload the splendor of Chinese take-out. Make mine light. So, how was your day?"

"It made the list of the Top Ten Shittiest. How about you?"

"Workin' the streets, bustin' tourists, and druggies. Lookin' for pimps and dealers who can lead us up the supply chain. My dad used to say sometimes work was like pushing a peanut with your nose the entire length of the Grand Concourse—slow and painful with nothing to show for your efforts at the end of the day except dirt that doesn't wash off. Today I did the entire Concourse, and all I got was the filth. Sit here and tell me what went wrong in your day."

She was patting the middle pillow on the couch. The offer was well received.

"First there was Chakika Washington's funeral. Back at the station, I get a call from some crackpot who claims to know all and will tell all for fifty large. Then I get an intrusion from some asshole, who claims to be from the *Post*. He begins to accuse me and the force of ignoring *The Information Man*. Obviously, we are, or I am, being set up by this pair. Who are they? And why now? I just want to crawl beneath my big bankie and hide until all this blows over. I want it to go away. Or I want it all out in the open, so I can fight it fair and square. God, I'm whining."

"Give me your hand. I'm going to squeeze all the shit out of your life for this evening. I don't know about tomorrow."

Her hands were strong and tender, the perfect expression of lover-friend-mother. She looked into Tony's eyes.

The magnets attracted. North and south poles glided inexorably toward a juncture of the lips. Mouths opened slightly to relieve the external pressure of two heads gently butting. Lips parted, but cheeks did not touch.

The memories rushed into Tony's head. The thousands of kisses over the decades were never this sweet, this caring. Separation was hesitant and very slow.

"I'm not sure what to say. I mean part of me has reacted. And my brain is whirring. As you promised, you lanced the boil of the day's anxiety. But I'm frightened. Frightened of what I want to do. Frightened of what this used to lead to. Frightened of what this could do to us. Face it, Magee, when I went clean, I got scared, because I was able to discern right from wrong."

"Relax, I'm a big girl. You're a big boy. What I want doesn't have to hurt either one of us. I'm not looking for a long-term commitment. Just tonight. Let's eat and talk. Then you can decide. Dinner consists of moo goo gai pan, sweet and sour pork, and shrimp egg rolls. Plus, gelatto for dessert. Sit here while I dish out the dinner."

"Shit. I almost forgot. I have to make a long-distance

phone call. I'll pay you for the charges. Can I use the phone in your bedroom?"

"That's great. I can't get you in my bedroom, but the telephone can. Sure, help yourself."

Tony dialed the new number for Special Agent Rissi. At the sixth ring, Rissi answered.

"Hello, Agent Rissi, this is Tony Sattill calling as you asked."

"Fine. Now give me your number, and I'll call you right back. Security you know."

In less than a minute Magee's phone rang. After telling her it was for him, Tony picked up on the sixth ring.

"You are on a secure landline. That's good. Now listen carefully. Wilson and Weaver of your force told Elija Washington to back off Road Developers. They signed all the forms. NYPD led the investigation. State police and the FBI were there just for assistance, credit, and to assume responsibility for any expansion of jurisdiction. Also, to make sure there were no major screw ups, like local investigators being compromised. So, if I were you, I would forget about everyone but Washington, Wilson, and Weaver. My notes indicate the investigation was expanded to include the bank management, but I don't know who. The bank executives seemed to be in lock step with Road Developers and the hidden power of the company. My notes further indicate that your state police and I were repeatedly denied access to complete information about the facts of the case and the people being investigated. I thought that NYPD was afraid we would steal their thunder, so they played it close to the vest.

Maybe they were covering something or someone. Inter-agency investigations are the pits. They are so territorial. So Balkanized. There is rarely the cooperation that the public thinks. That's all I know, and that's all I want to know. Good-bye Detective Sattill. Good luck. And be cautious."

The click of Special Agent Rissi's phone preceded the click of Tony's micro-recorder by five seconds. Tony had to pretend the phone call meant nothing while he tried to control what would or would not happen this evening.

"Well, *Secret Agent Man*, you look like shit. Either my holistic squeeze treatment didn't work, or the call was a toxin too powerful for just a hand job. Maybe you need a full body squeeze."

"Magee, I am digging much deeper into the compost heap, and it is beginning to scare the rot out of me. Thus, the wan skin."

"Look before we enjoy the meal, upon which I slaved for seconds, we need to talk. Perhaps, unburdening yourself would help. If there is stuff you can't tell me, it's okay. But the more you tell—the more you share—the lighter your load. Look, we've known each other for decades, warts and all. We know each other well beyond the biblical definition. We've seen parts of our respective bodies and psyches that no one else will ever see. Let's put the evening's festivities on hold for the time being and talk.

From Captain Brainerd's assignment to Special Agent Rissi's phone call, Tony went into the amount of detail he deemed safe. Some information was too speculative to share at this time. While he was talking, he decided to send copies of all the hard data and files on a flash drive to Franklin Ranck, his lawyer. One could never have enough insurance. The words and thoughts flowed out of him. Sometimes in a sputter, sometimes in a gush. Speaking helped to codify and connect the events and facts, however disjointed or separated by time. Tony even made a few observations and drew some conclusions, which were new. Magee did not interrupt. She just listened. The purging took thirty minutes, and it sapped him of the little strength remaining after the telephone call.

"Tony, I don't know what to make of all this. My instinct tells me it is an ancient rat's nest that should be left buried. My training tells me it is a current event about to surface like an island in the Pacific. In either case, it was yours and is now ours. I won't attempt to comment or offer words of great wisdom. I need time to think, review all the details, and see if I can determine where they could lead us. Yes, us. Two members of the same force. That's all—for now. You must eat something. I'll get the food."

After Tony inhaled the three Chinese offerings and the Italian palate cleanser, color returned to his cheeks.

He had to leave. Home and to bed. A good night's sleep so he could face Friday with its attendant road race. The kiss at the door was a repeat of the deep tenderness of the one on the couch.

This was good, very good. Too good, he feared.

The next day, Tony and Connie headed onto the pothole-riddled, first leg of the weekend's road rally. Departure time 6:25:30. ETA 8:47:30.

Grab the cash, celebrate and, humiliate.

Connie had settled in the rarely used back-seat. She had eviscerated her leather bag, and the papers and manila folders were strewn over the seat and floor. She had a ton of work to do before Monday's meeting with the financial gurus at Dunham & Treet, LLC. She had to read and understand the proposals. This preparation would also require numerous real-time and email discussions with her partners during the weekend. As a result of her preoccupation, the couple would not couple. Tony had been put on hiatus before.

∽∾∽∾

Agent Rissi was about a hundred yards from the dock. This had been a good day for fishing—two meal-sized Lake Trout, one for tonight, one for the freezer. Solitary fishing had become a ritual for Tom. Angela had no interest whatsoever in sitting in a small boat and waiting for the fish to give it up.

His wife of his life would not clean or cook the fish. She would, however, devour the fruits of Tom's other love—and even prepare the side dishes and clean up after the meal…sometimes. This division of labor had existed for decades.

∽∾∽∾

The trip down the West Side Highway was particularly problematic today. A major fender bender delayed Tony fifteen minutes. The poor suckers behind him would be held up a minimum of thirty minutes as a result of the fire trucks and wreckers trying to extricate the gnarled metal mess from the left lane. The good side of the accident was that traffic in front of it was almost sparse. Sparse enough for Tony to regain two minutes prior to the tunnel and a total of eight before the Turnpike. He was closing in on par. Connie was shuffling papers, digging into the bag, flipping through the four of five stacks, making notes on a legal pad—all of which would be entered into her laptop when she was at The Bluffs.

ဢၢ

The fisherman pulled slowly on the oars. No engine for the boat, just like no barbs on the hooks. To Tom fishing was an art. The less science and the fewer modern enhancements, the better the experience. Pure fishing would be with his hands. Maybe he'd get there someday. The lake looked smooth enough to walk on. But Tom deferred that event to Christ. The dipping splash of the oars was echoed in the splash of the birds diving to feed on this late afternoon. Bugs on the water's surface seduced the fish to leave the safety of the lake's bottom. They rose to feed. The birds hovering above the bugs dove to feed on the fish. A symbiotic relationship and a perfect example of the food chain. Tom wondered if the bugs were ever eaten by the fish before the birds got there. Or did the bugs live to trick again? Closer to the dock he rowed. There was no real urgency.

⊘⊘⊘

Once on the Turnpike, Tony forced the car into the left lane and started the game of follow-the-leader. He wanted to take control and lead. The traffic was building with each mile marker. He had to make up time. He had to win this weekend. Connie was lost in the plans for her future.

"C, do you mind if I crank up the tunes?"

"Uh, okay. Just not too loud. I've got to ingest all this material by tomorrow when the seven of us conference."

Flashing lights of two cruisers are evident ahead. Another accident? Another slow down for sure. Another attempt to catch up. This time it was a mother with screaming kids and a flat tire. Two troopers were there to protect and change the tire. Traffic roared around the three-car hump. Tony was too slowly gaining on par. Traffic thickened like soup into stew.

⊘⊘⊘

A few more strokes and the boat bumped casually against the piling. Tom hugged the post to tie up, bow and aft. His rod and tackle box were lifted to the dock. The fish trap was pulled from the water and drained. The bounty bucket was placed next to the tackle box. Tom hoisted himself onto the weather-worn and warped planks that were his pier. He gathered up all his belongings, heaved a sigh of relief, and plodded up the hill to his home. It had been a good day. What could be bad about fishing and napping? Time of day, age, and relative inactivity had made him tired. More tired than he would have been before retirement. The sun's warmth was diminishing. Shadows foretold the night. A large gray misshapen version of Tom ambled to the lakefront home.

⌘

The entrance to the Garden State Parkway was jammed. Probably someone without change in the Exact Change Lane. On to the last venue to compensate for the time lag, which was now four minutes. This could be made up by going ninety-five. No big deal.

"How are we doing on time, sweetie?"

"We'll make it, thanks to my expert use of the accelerator and the fact that I have not braked, except for tolls, since we left the tunnel. I think we can win this week, if the damned bridge is not raised to let the drunks into port. How are you coming?"

"There is so much to understand. Past, present, and future. And so little time. The pressure is severe. Each little decision will greatly impact everything thereafter. I hate this part of business. Why can't somebody do this for me?"

"Because it's your company."

"Shut up and drive, Anthony. I hate it when you're right, and I'm lost."

☙☙☙

The angler deposited the rod and tackle box on the back porch and entered the house through the kitchen. He retrieved his boning knife and a baggie with a tie for the guts and outer parts of the catch. Tom headed for the hose for the messy part of the day. Both fish were ready for cooking. One was wrapped in freezer paper. The entrée of the evening was laid in a covered dish with herbs and breadcrumbs. This would chill during Tom's shower and first cocktail. Angela had been reading her latest adult mystery and nodding off as her pre-cocktail nap. Tom did not disturb her as he headed to the shower to wash away the stink of sweat in old clothes and freshly caught fish. Clean and redressed, he headed to the living room and kissed Angela awake. Another ritual. She stirred, stretched, and kissed him back.

☙☙☙

In the rearview mirror, Tony noticed car lights flashing. Keeping one eye on the traffic in front and one eye on the traffic to the right, he tried to search the driver's side and determine who is signaling him.

"Hey, business exec. Can you take a break from your minutia and look behind at the asshole who's flashing us?"

"Well, speedy, it's Red and Babs in one of their bookend autos. I wonder when they started and where they are in timing. They are moving over to the right and are about to force their way around us. Don't let the king and queen of Jersey get ahead."

"Relax, the road rally is based on precise ETA, and according to my official police force chronometer, we are about two minutes behind our schedule to win."

The Mercedes pulled alongside. Red flashed the international single-digit salute of disdain and cut in front of Tony. The duck-in was acceptable by the code of reckless abandoned ethics because there were less than two car lengths—much less. But there was nothing Tony could do, except stay the course and arrive precisely on time. First toll ahead.

☙☙☙

Bourbon and ginger for Angela and Scotch on the rocks for Tom—silent communication a by-product of years of love and understanding.

"How was your piscatorial excursion?"

"Two nice-sized. I'll save one for when the Durwards come over next week. I'll catch a second one for that night day after tomorrow. How's the book?

"No too bad. A little bloody. Very intricate. Style is refreshing. It's a new author, some young man named Andes. When do you plan on starting dinner?"

"I'll fire up the stove in about thirty minutes. Now, I want to relax and stare at my love."

"Will you still need me, will you still feed me, when I'm sixty-four?"

෩෩

Red and Tony seemed to be moving in tandem. Snaking in and out of traffic, they arrived at the Exact Change Booth and exited as one. Red paid for both cars. The blinking lights went still five seconds after Tony's exit. Like a V-1 rocket, Red's coup left Tony's sedan struggling to reach illegal speed.

"Hurry, they're getting ahead. And can you keep it steady, my papers are sliding all over the place back here?"

"We're on schedule. I don't know or care about him. If we arrive too early, we lose. There is no sense in making this a two-car race. Besides I can't control the pitching a yawing if I go much faster or weave too much. And I certainly don't want to make a mess of your paper stacks."

"Fuck you and your testosterone road rally, just drive."

He could see the lights of the second and last toll booth on the horizon. And he noted what had to be Red's coupe nearly flying toward the entrance to the exit of this leg.

෩෩

Tom arose from the easy chair of a thousand memories and headed to his appointed place in the kitchen.

"Dear, I'd be careful of the burners," Angela said. "I'm not sure they're working properly. Gave me fits this morning."

Tom opened the refrigerator door and extracted the elements of the evening's meal: fish, fresh green beans, and potato au gratin. About thirty minutes of prep time and onto the table. He turned on the oven and inserted the Pyrex dish with the potatoes, cut the beans and got a frying pan out for the fish. No flame from the burner. Tom reached in the door to the right of the stove, found the big box of Ohio Blue Tips, and struck one.

❈

Beneath the hood of Red's Rocket, a pinhole in the hose leading to the primary power steering pump became a hole, then became a crack, and then split the hose in half. All within two seconds. The fluid spewed throughout the engine compartment as the power steering system tightened up. The hose to the auxiliary pump popped from its coupling, and more fluid misted over the hot engine head and block. The steering wheel nearly locked up. Red exerted substantial energy just to keep the missile in line with the toll lane. The explosion of smoke and steam burst from under the hood with such force that the metal canopy crashed into the windshield. Red instinctively slammed on the brakes as acrid dark air flowed into the front of the car's cabin. The car weaved in and out of the lane because Red couldn't see or steer. All was panic and confusion. Red was homing in on the concrete-block structure that separated the lanes. The impact of unstoppable projectile and immovable target sent flames skyward twenty feet. Other cars followed. The entire event was over in thirty seconds. The mélange of metal, rubber, fabric, flesh, and flames halted traffic for hours. Jersey *Caca pasa.*

℮ჯℯჯ

The fireball emanating from the kitchen stove measured more than 15,000 cubic feet. The house measured 12,000 cubic feet. The explosion drove Tom's fragmented body through two walls and onto the front porch. Angela went through one wall and onto the front yard. Her head landed near the water, three feet from Tom's. The house went from structure to splinters to inferno in about two seconds. Nothing was left, except angry shards of kitchen appliances, bathroom tubs, and the flagstone around the fireplace. The remains looked like a Kosovar palace. Fire investigators determined that one of the hoses feeding gas to the stove must have come loose. Must have happened when Peninsular Gas delivered the three extra tanks and hooked them up in sequence.

Retirement *Caca pasa.*

CHAPTER 7

160 West 18th Street:

Brainerd left an early morning yellow-sticky-on-the-telephone message that there would be an important meeting at nine a.m. with Mr. Wallace of the *Post*, and Tony's presence was required.

"Captain, what is the meeting all about?"

"We're going to explain to Mr. Wallace exactly how we feel about this alleged informant and Mr. Wallace's involvement in the obvious shakedown. It seems some of your brothers in blue did some real detective work and found out that the two gentlemen in question are close associates. Asshole buddies, ya' might say. We want to put a stop to this interference with our investigation."

"Sir, will it just be you and I doing the talking?"

"Well, laddy, I will talk. You'll be listenin' and learnin'."

At ten after nine, the desk sergeant rang Brainerd's office. As he headed toward one of the interview rooms, the captain waved for Tony to follow. Wallace was rumpled in his faded green pullover, dirty khaki pants, and scuffed shoes. He sported the stubble of a beard, and his hair was matted as if unshampooed for a few days. He looked the part of the tireless reporter. Sitting at the table facing the blank wall, his diminutive stature corroborated his insignificance. His shoulders were barely nine inches above the tabletop.

"Mr. Wallace of the *Post*, I am Captain Brainerd, and this is Detective Sattill of the New York Police Department. The purpose of this meeting is to discuss your involvement in the so-called Handyman Murders. Before we let you ask any questions, let me tell you what we know. You don't know jack shit. You are on a fishing expedition to enhance your stature at the paper and the media in general as the one who cracked the Handyman Murders. So, you set up an alleged informant to hold out the hope of information, knowing full well that he only knows what you know, which is zippo. Your goal is to get the NYPD to jump through hoops to protect its collective ass. Maybe we'll even leak some information, which you can print for a by-line on page three. Well, since you know nothing, and we won't tell you anything, you're shit out of luck. So, stop this silly exercise and tell your informant to quit bothering us.

"Now, Mr. Wallace, let us ask you two questions.

One, do you have your editor's approval for your unprofessional dirty work? You'll notice I didn't say unethical or illegal because you have not yet sunk to one of those levels. And when you sleep with your informant, who is on the top? By the by, we know the answers already. Now, do have any questions for us?"

Despite the stubble and dirt, Wallace's face had turned ashen. His dainty hands were trembling, but his eyes burned with strength borne of fear and hatred.

"Listen Captain Brainless, and you too, Defective Sattill," he hissed. "As a reporter, I don't need any approval to investigate a story, particularly a police department fuck-up. Plus, my sex life is my own business. So, fuck off."

"Sir, do yourself a favor and drop this entire charade. If you choose to pursue this hopeless cause, I will personally destroy you and your lover. Remember that I know you, where you live, and what you do. It only takes a second to pick up the phone and call your editor. Or we'll tail you to those sleazy leather-and-fist-fucking bars. Bust the bars and make sure your name is prominently displayed on the police blotter of the *News* and page three of the *Post*. Now leave my station."

"You haven't heard the last of me, Captain." Wallace slithered down the hall and stairs.

Kelly and Echlebaum exited the door from the side viewing room and left the station-house by the back door.

"That, laddy, is how you attack a viper. Aggressively. Notice how I got in the little bugger's face and never blinked. Now, what can you tell me about Elija Washington?"

"Captain, I'll have the report on your desk within a week. There are a few loose ends I have to follow."

Tony looked for his mug. He wanted coffee. No mug. Must have mislaid it somewhere in the building. Not an uncommon event. Happened at least three times a month. He searched, gave up. Someone called to tell him where his beloved Brown University mug had strayed. It was a running joke. Tony even thought guys took it and hid it just to rib him. *Time to use the auxiliary Franklin & Marshall mug.* Where coffee was concerned, it was good to be prepared. He settled in to scan the *Post* and *News*. A blurb in The Nation Section caught his attention.

Fire Ravages Peninsula. Traverse City, MI. A wildfire consumed twenty-five acres of the Upper Peninsula of Michigan. The blaze apparently started in home of retired FBI Special Agent Thomas Rissi and his wife of forty years, Angela. The house was completely destroyed. Investigators speculate that the fire was the result of a faulty connection in the gas line leading to the stove. Both adults perished in the explosion and inferno, which followed.

A solitary bead of sweat trickled down Tony's neck, and a knot grew in his stomach. The sense that something was moving out of the shadows and closer to him was very strong.

Rissi. Never met the man. Spoke to him twice. Asked some questions and got some answers. Died in a non-accident. I got him killed. By whom? Why? Red and

Babs. Knew them well. Spent summers with them. Red was dirty once, but not now. They died in an automobile accident. Or was it intentional destruction. By whom? Why? Is there a connection between the deaths of the Rissis and the Saylors? There has to be a line of filament that is invisible to the casual looker. Why can't I see it? Is there a connection between the deaths of Jenks and Washington? Are there connections, other than cosmic, between all of the recent deaths? Yes or no. If no, stop. If yes, what? Who? Why? What do I have to do with all the death and destruction? Am I the cause? Am I the reason all these people are now dead? When will the police force step into the sunlight?

The arrangements for the Saylors had been made by Red's law firm. Another funeral. Another email invitation. Wednesday at ten a.m. at Holy Redeemer Church, 110 West Central Avenue in Englewood. *Call Connie. Ask Brainerd for time lost.* Now there were four.

Tony dove into the sea of paperwork to drown his anxiety.

Dinner at Elija's tonight would be arduous. Tony arrived precisely at six-thirty p.m.

"Tony, it's nice to see you. How long has it been?"

Elija's eyes were red-rimmed from crying, and his shoulders were stooped from the pressure of death, explanations to a child, and planning for an unsure future. He gestured politely for Tony to enter.

"Elija, if this isn't a good time for you, we can do it later."

"No, Tony, now is the best time. The sooner we discuss what we have to discuss, the better I'll feel. Would you like a drink? I'm having a nice '92 Merlot."

"That sounds expensive and perfect."

Elija led Tony through the foyer, dining room and kitchen, and out onto the balcony. The living room where his wife had been brutalized was off limits. The French doors were closed and probably locked. Tony would see some shreds of the ever-so-sorry police tape on the floor in the living room. There was room enough for four chairs and a small table on the balcony. Tony sat while Elija pours.

"Where is Byron?"

"In his room. Let me get him. Byron, could you come out here for a second? I'd like you to meet an old friend."

The teenage boy entered the doorway. His face was a carbon copy of his mother's. His build was greater than Elija's. Elija could remember Chakika for all time by looking into Byron's eyes. The boy showed no signs of the tragedy as he bounced up to Tony and extended his hand.

"Hello, Byron, I'm Tony Sattill, a friend of your parents. How ya doin'?"

"Fine, I guess, given the circumstances, I mean. Maybe it will really sink in soon. Are you with the force, too?"

"Yes, but I'm a friend of your dad's first."

"Do you guys mind if I go back to my computer?"

"Not at all. It's nice to meet you. Take care of yourself."

"He is seeing a grief therapist, who was recommended by the force. Maybe I should see one, also. Maybe later. Now that the amenities and introductions are over, and the warmth of the wine is beginning to work, let's talk. Tony, I know you've been investigating my investigation into Road Developers. I don't know who directed you to dig, why, what you've learned, or what you've surmised. But I think it's important for me to come clean to you, my friend. I want you to know my side of the story before erroneous assumptions are made, and inappropriate actions are taken. So, let's conduct this discussion like a Q and A session during a deposition. You ask, and I'll respond."

"That's refreshingly candid. But why a Q and A format?"

"In this format, I can give you exactly the information you ask for. I can confirm or deny facts or leads. This format also lets me help you without hurting myself. I become a witness or an informant rather than a conspirator. By the way, if you are wearing a wire, the evening is over right now. Are you wearing a wire?"

"First, the format is your choice since I am seeking the information and don't wish to harm you. Second, I am not wearing a wire."

Wearing a wire—no. Carrying a tape recorder—yes. Elija didn't ask about a micro-recorder.

"Who gave you permission to initiate the investigation?"

"I met with Lieutenant Patrick Lynch of the two-four. He laid out the scenario for me. There had been complaints of bid-fixing and sub-contractor intimidation. Two guys had had their trucks burn up. Told me I was chosen to lead the investigation. The feds and the state police would function as advisors. It was pretty much grab-ass from my standpoint. I begged, borrowed, and stole man-hours from every available guy that was looking to earn points with the brass. I thought, at the time, the force wanted me to succeed. Now, I know they wanted me on the investigation because they could benefit from my success and not be dirtied by my failure. I was a poster boy. I understand that Lynch was promoted to Captain after the investigation was closed. He retired a month later and drowned in Long Island Sound on Memorial Day, two months after that."

"During the investigation, who were your handlers?"

"Lynch bowed out after the initial meet and Lieutenants Boyd Wilson and Jack Weaver were introduced as my bosses at the local level. Byers and Slotkin from the state police and Special Agent Tom Rissi of the FBI. The state and federal people gave me a wide berth like aunts and uncles. Everything they did had to go through Wilson and Weaver, my parents."

"Did you or your wife receive money from the First Bank of Long Island?"

"No."

"Did your wife receive money from Road Developers?"

"Yes. Chakika was paid for consulting services to Road Developers. Checks were made out to CM Enterprises."

"How much money did you receive?"

"In excess of four hundred fifty thousand dollars over a five-year period."

"Who at the bank authorized the deposit of company or corporate checks into a personal account?"

"Gene Eichelberger, president of the bank."

"How else was Mr. Eichelberger connected to the investigation?"

"Mr. Eichelberger was Lieutenant Wilson's stepfather. He married Lieutenant Wilson's mother a few years after Mr. Eichelberger's first wife died. I believe Wilson must have been a small child when the second marriage occurred."

"What is Alphonse Mirtan's involvement in the payments?"

"As a substantial customer of the bank, both personal and business—he was an executive with Road Developers—Mr. Mirtan facilitated the transactions."

"Were the payments to your wife discussed with you as being anything other than fee for service?"

"No."

"On what exactly did your wife consult?"

"I cannot recall."

"Did your wife meet with members of Road Developers for business purposes?"

"She told me, yes. On numerous occasions, she traveled to the bank for meetings with her client."

"Did you attend any of these meetings?"

"No."

"At what point did the fee for service payments cease?"

"As I look back on the timeline, the payments ended when the mortgage, held by the bank, was paid off and about three months before the investigation was stopped."

"To your knowledge, were any of the other members of your investigative team or their spouses receiving fee-for-service payments?"

"No."

"To your knowledge, were any of your supervisors, local, state, and federal receiving fee-for-service payments."

"No."

"Do you suspect any of your team, your supervisors, or their spouses of receiving fee-for-service payments?"

"Yes. I suspect that Wilson and Weaver somehow received money from either the bank or Road Developers through the bank. But I can't prove this suspicion."

"Did you ever meet with bank officials during the course of your investigation?"

"No. At first, I didn't want to let them know they were part of the investigation. Then, when I suggested digging into the bank's records, Weaver steered me elsewhere. Down a few blind alleys. Auto dealerships. Furniture rental stores. Household contractors. He said he needed federal approval to dig into the bank, and that the feds were not readily forthcoming with that. So, he would handle it through channels. I took that to mean he would get back to me. He never did. By the time I realized he had stalled me, the case was ordered closed."

"Who ordered the case closed?"

"I was told the FBI and the state saw no future in the case and recommended to the commanders and the chief that it should be shut down. When I asked Special Agent Rissi, he said that Wilson and Weaver had closed the case because it was going nowhere and costing too many man-hours and too much money. As I look back on the events of the time, I was concerned that Wilson and Weaver were constantly and tightly monitoring my every move, my every request, and my every inquiry. I had to be de-briefed daily toward the end. At the beginning of the investigation, they just wanted weekly written reports for their files."

"Do you know of anyone who would want to kill Special Agent Rissi?"

"No. Well, maybe Wilson and Weaver, because his story would conflict with theirs if someone ever asked both parties."

"Do you think there was a cover-up?"

"Yes."

"How was Wilson involved in the cover-up?"

"Via his stepfather, Eichelberger, is my guess."

"How was Weaver involved in the cover-up?"

"Not sure. He was hooked to Road Developers somehow. Can we take a meal break, now? I'm hungry, the wine bottle is empty, and I want to feed Byron."

"Sure. I'd like to freshen up. Then I'll help with dinner."

"The bathroom is off to the left past the living room."

Taking care of personal hygiene allowed Tony time to change the tape in the micro-recorder. This was getting very clear in some areas and raising lots of questions elsewhere. The dinner, consisting of London Broil, baked potatoes, and green beans and sliced tomatoes in vinaigrette, seemed to be comfort food for Byron. He had seconds on everything, grabbed a Klondike Bar, and headed back to his room. He never shut the door. Nothing to hide, and he did not want to lose touch with his dad.

"Leave the dishes, and let the grill and pots soak. The maid will get them. She comes tomorrow. I think I'll ask her if she wants to move into the third bedroom. Be a live-in for us. I need someone to watch over the house while I'm out. Byron starts college in a few weeks. He's going to St Johns. Got a computer science scholarship. The boy is a genius. He set up both computer systems, his and my personal one. I couldn't wire a Christmas tree, and he has us hooked to each other. My only concern is that he may be too good for his own good. I think he and his buddies may have hacked into confidential systems and files. No proof, just a hunch about his teen thing. Now, where were we?"

"Do you know Captain Brainerd?"

"Your uncle? Sure. A good man. Perhaps a little wrapped up in police force politics, but which dinosaur isn't?"

"Have you ever had any official dealings with Captain Brainerd?"

"No."

"Do you know of any reason he would want to know more about you?"

"Not really. I think he knows I was the lead on the Road Developers' investigation. He's pals with Wilson and Weaver. I would think he would ask them."

"Do you have any idea who might have wanted to harm your wife?"

"No. I mean, we both know who my father-in-law is and his connection to the mob on Long Island. But why would anyone want to kill her?"

"I don't know. I'm asking the questions. You tell me."

The respondent was trying to be the interrogator.

"Do you think somebody is trying to send me a message?"

"Maybe. I don't know who, or what they're trying to tell you. I mean you already canned the investigation. Do you think the murder could be a message to your father-in-law?"

"It could. But why?"

"Do you think Benedetto and his boys are sending a signal to Alphonse, to shut up?"

"They could."

"Do you think the message to shut up could also be coming from anyone else?"

"Who?"

"You tell me."

"Maybe Wilson, based on his connection with the bank. I don't know about Weaver because I don't know his dirty connection. That said, I am certain those two are joined at the wallet and hip."

"Why did you enter the file after the investigation was closed?"

"CYA. I wanted to make damned sure that if the case were ever re-opened, and somebody determined there were major screw-ups, I would take others with me when I went down. What I can't understand is that why that stuff has remained in the file these past years. I mean, why has no one erased my entry?"

"I can guess numerous reasons. First, no one looked to see if the files were altered because they felt it was safe. Or, if they looked, the fact that you entered the file and revised it would show up on the electronic log. Also, their entry to spy on you would be registered on the log. Entries can't be erased or explained away easily. Last, if someone did look, they would realize that you probably had back-up stashed away for your own protection. One can never have enough life insurance. In other words, they didn't think about it, because they didn't want to know the answer."

"Did you notice any file entries after mine?"

Tony shook his head. "No, but I haven't checked in the last three weeks." The respondent was trying to be the interrogator again. "Do you think your wife was having an affair?" Tony asked.

"What the fuck kind of question is that?"

"Just part of the Q and A. Were you having an affair?"

"Well, Chakika and I may have had our normal difficulties in the early years of our marriage, but we were straight with each other. There were no problems. And no others."

"Sorry to be so intrusive, but I had to ask. Has anyone contacted you since the murder?"

"Who do you mean by anyone?"

"Anyone out of the ordinary—like Wilson or Weaver—like Eichelberger—like someone from SIU."

"No."

"Do you have the feeling your activities are under scrutiny? Is anybody watching you?"

"Not that I'm sure of. But you'll notice that tonight I won't talk about anything important in the house. Just out here. This whole mess has me worried that somebody may be listening."

"Would you turn over your personal file for my scrutiny?"

"No. That's why it's called personal."

"Elija, I am nearly talked out. You've been a great help. I don't want to intrude anymore this evening. If I think of anything else I want to ask, I'll call. And, if there's anything I should know, please call me. Now, I'd better head for home."

The two men shook hands at the door. Tony yelled goodnight to Byron and received a favorable response. In the cab weaving its way up Madison Avenue, Tony concluded that either he confirmed large hunks of the truth or he was just conned by a pro. Elija must have something to hide beyond the money. Besides, the connection to the fee was tenuous. Maybe Chakika earned the money. Was the Q and A format the easiest way for Elija to unburden his soul or practice for a nasty team of investigators like Kelly and Echlebaum? Two questions remained—how much was true and how much should he tell Brainerd?

The morning was filled with forms. Tony qualified to carry the new Glock. He turned in his old .32, secured his new cannon, and acquired one hundred rounds of ammunition. He kept two clips on him at all times and a spare clip at home.

It was funeral day. This could become quite a distasteful routine. Seven people were dead in less than a month. What was wrong with this picture? He drove to Englewood. His Mazda would fit inside the trunk of some of the stretch limos outside the church. The men were just a little too somber, and the women were crying just a little too much. There were no kids. This was a grown-up performance. Two small urns on an altar in front of the railing. Lots of dark red candles had driven up the temperature in the church seven to ten degrees. The clothes on the active performers depicted how important they thought others should think they were. Men's suits were in the $1500 range. The women's dresses were in the $2500 range, with shoes to make Imelda jealous. He and Connie were woefully underdressed. The priest gave a ten-minute sermon on the virtue of service to mankind. The entire performance was considerately brief. Tony and Connie were invited to a reception at a private home. He politely declined the invitation over Connie's mild protestation. They knew so few of the guests, and there was no family.

Connie was stone cold in thought on the way home. No tears, just silence.

"Whatchya' thinkin' about, C?"

"Lots of stuff, given where we came from. I mean, they had their lives ahead of them, just like we do. Now they're gone. We could be gone in an instant. How do we protect ourselves from a quick and deadly accident? What do we do to preserve our lives?"

"Nothing, except to be careful. We can't preserve that over which we have little or no control. That which has been given to us can be taken away."

"That sounds suspiciously Catholic. I can't buy into that without question. Why would God destroy Red and Babs or allow them to be destroyed? What were they in his plan?"

"You are asking me to decipher the will of God, a will I have been trained to take on faith. I can only view the workings of God's will on a post facto basis. I can never anticipate his actions, because, if I could, I would be as omniscient as the creator of the universe. This can never be. Christ, his son, could not anticipate God's actions. Christ accepted God's actions."

Connie was staring straight ahead.

"I don't want to road rally anymore. I am afraid of the risk. Call off the race."

There was no race. Just an extremely moribund weekend.

CHAPTER 8

One Police Plaza:

Just as the bowels were a doctor's treasure trove of answers to ailment mysteries, so too the police department's library tombs were the best place to look for the truth. Magee had joined Tony on his adventure into the cave of facts and revealed knowledge. With her probative intellect at the ready, she passed through the various security checkpoints with ease. The pair head for the elevator designated basement levels. The basement levels housed hard copy, ancient and detailed. The information in the files had been summarized for reference and was on the mainframe files. Often the files were so old that nobody cared a damn about what was in them.

Arriving at Level 1, they searched the discreet computer for any files relating to Road Developers and First

Bank of Long Island. This was a start. Later they would probe the multilevel fortress for information about Wilson, Weaver, Eichelberger, Lynch, Washington, and Brainerd.

Files pertaining to Road Developers were designated II-2-4-79-A-3, II-2-5-86-B-2, III-2-3-50-B-1, and III-3-5-87-A-1. Files pertaining to First Bank of Long Island were designated I-1-7-60-A-4, II-7-6-94-B-2, and III-8-3-45-B-1. The filing system was based on chronology. The oldest were on the first level and the newer files were down on Levels II and III. When the three levels were filled, the oldest files were destroyed. This occurred every fifteen-to-twenty years. The designations for file placement were Floor, Area—Aisle, Row and Gondola—Panel of the Gondola, and Shelf. The individual files were in large ubiquitous Banker's Boxes. The size of the boxes dictated that, if a file did not fill a box, the box was "filled" with another or other files. The NYPD conserved space. Tony had to find each box containing the right file and drag the box to a reading table. Magee suggested that they start with the file closest at hand: First Bank on Level I-Aisle 1-Row 7-Gondola 60-Panel A-Shelf 4. The boxes could not be filed on the shelves alphabetically by subject because the subjects were mixed within boxes. This meant that hunting for the right box was time-consuming.

Of course, over time the files and the boxes had been removed and put back anywhere on the original shelf, panel, gondola, row, aisle, or floor. In other words, there was always a good chance that the file sought was anywhere in the basement, just not where it was supposed to be. The search started.

Initial success, except that the box was mixed with the Gs on shelf five, well above Tony's head. Two aisles over, he found a library ladder and dragged it where the two seekers needed it. The reading table was two aisles over the other way, and the fluorescent bulb was flickering. Inside the box was a small folder labeled First Bank of Long Island: Case No.: 82-7878. In the same box were three files labeled with three different defendants.

"Looks like a mass of forms and corporate papers. Why would the NYPD have a file of this? The case at hand must have started out civil, and become criminal. Names, addresses, legal documents, and signatures. A suit was brought by a neighborhood association, which felt it was being redlined out of loans. There were some threats and property damage. Allegedly a house was torched. The bank was picketed to up the ante. The case went to court but was dropped. The association agreed to accept payment of two hundred fifty thousand dollars and not discuss or pursue the matter further. A new house was built for the association president. No contractor name."

"Well, Magee, we have our first piece of historical non-evidence, from which we can only surmise…nothing."

"I bet the house was built by Road Developers. Maybe it's how they got their dirty feet in the bank's door. They volunteered to be a good citizen, then made deposits into and sought loans from the bank they had helped. Ultimately the company and its management became important customers of the bank. From this position, they were able to exert power over bank operations. Ingeniously insidious."

"We have three files on Level Two and three more on Level Three. You choose the next stop."

"Level Two. We're on a roll. Let's try to keep this in a time sequence. From the past to the present. Why are we whispering?"

"We are whispering because we are concerned that we may be heard by someone. It's a common reaction when one is in a library or the stacks of a library. These catacombs remind us both of college library stacks. My experience was in Providence. I remember yours was in Philadelphia. Since there is no one here to hear us, we can speak in normal tones."

"No, we should continue to whisper. I have this feeling we are being monitored. Don't spin around, but there is a small camera at the end of each aisle and one near the reading table. We are being visually monitored for sure. Our probe into the system to get the file locations would be noted by anyone who reads the log. Face it, Tony, we are not alone."

Tony bent over, ostensibly to lace his shoe, and spotted the cameras. He ejected a loud whisper. "Fuck me."

"Not here, we'd be videoed, and my moaning might be recorded. It is a great idea, but later, at my apartment is a better place."

"Seriously, whoever is looking or listening must know by now who we are and why we're here. We should go about our business as if we are not aware of their presence."

"Tony, I doubt if anyone will see or hear us in real time. I suspect, rather, that the entire place is monitored, and the computer, audio, and video records are held for a period of time for possible review. If the monitoring records are not needed by the authorities, the media are erased and reused. Or maybe everything is just filed away. You know records of records of records. Bureaucracy at its best."

Down to the Second Canto of Hell. Three files on this level: two for Road Developers and one for First Bank. The folders for Road Developers looked like they had been picked over by the censor vultures. Pages were missing. One document contained pages one, four, six, and nine. It was a safe bet there were entire documents missing. The total amount of material in the first box was sparse, to say the least. The box contained more empty space than paper. Box one contained a case dealing with alleged sub-contractor extortion. The two sides were told to "make nice" and play outside in the sunshine. Could the judiciary be involved with Road Developers? Money could make friends at any level. Box two dealt with unfair bidding practices. Road Developers was the plaintiff this time. Some schlep of a county commissioner tried to slide some business away from RD to one of his pals. RD blew the whistle. The commissioner got canned, the other contractor got banned, and RD got the job with an inflated bid or extensive overruns. Nothing like making a profit from the legal system.

What was interesting was that some of the names on the RD files were different in the second case. It appeared as if the company was trying to cleanse its face of mob acne and embellish its complexion with the foundation and rouge of respectability.

Old "goombas" were gone, and Alphonse Mirtan, Eugene Eichelberger, and Jacob Weaver were now part of the family. Was Jacob Jack's father? A safe bet. Why didn't Washington make that connection? Maybe he did but just forgot to tell Tony. If that was the case, what else did Washington forget in his "confession"? Was everything he told the truth? Not likely.

The First Bank box contained a very flat and very meager folder. Legal Cover Sheet only—Benedetto v First Bank of Long Island. *Wonder what shit the bank stepped into this time? How much or what did it cost the bank to clean the caca from its Guccis? Enter the gloom of the Third Canto. Three boxes here also. Go to the last First Bank box first.*

As Magee slid the library ladder to the appropriate aisle and gondola, she climbed and adjusted the camera away from the search area.

"Don't you think that's a little late? I mean, our itinerary is logged onto the main file, we are already on tape from the floors above, and now you think we can disguise what we are looking for. I thought you were smarter than that."

"I am. I just like to mess with their minds. This will cause them confusion if the tape is reviewed."

Tony climbed to the top and extracted the box from

the shelf. "Hey, it's empty except for the file we need. And the file is thick. We caught a break. Now we'll learn something."

"Easy, boy, it's not Christmas yet. Let's not go to the table. Open the box here, and we'll examine the treasure of *terra policia*."

Tony eased the box to the floor, leaped from the third step, lifted the lid, and leaned into the rectangle opening all in one fluid motion. Magee was behind him as he spread out the sheets to get a real overview of the case. Eugene Eichelberger, president of First Bank of Long Island, was convicted of embezzlement and fraud. Sentenced to fifteen years at the State Penitentiary at Ossining—Sing Sing. It seemed an anonymous informant provided forged bank transactions and copies of the true documents. The case never went to trial. Eichelberger confessed and made partial restitution. He should still be up the river. Tony made a note to question him.

In all his excitement at uncovering some kernel of historical matter, Tony only now sensed the warm, measured breath on the back of his neck. The dainty lip touching—not kissing. From one side of his neck to the other. From the collar of his shirt to the base of his skull. Magee's touch retraced the paths. She moved forward to mouth massage his neck and collar bones. Her hands slid around his rib cage and firmly gripped his pectoral muscles. She had joined him at the waist—her mons slowly ground his cheeks. Breathing was no longer measured, but had become deep and quivering.

He peeled away Magee's hands and turned to face

the love adversary of his life. Her stare told him every-thing and nothing at the same time. Lust fogged his vi-sion. And honest affection was smothered by flat-out, unmitigated lust. She grabbed the back of his head, locked his lips, and drove her tongue throughout his en-tire mouth. He followed her lead. Groping with buttons, belts, and zippers, they were naked and ready for the bat-tle of pleasure. The saliva on both intertwining tongues was thick with pre-coital excitement. Tony picked her up as she leaped and wrapped her arms around his neck. Coupling commenced. Dry discomfort slipped into warm, moist pleasure. The kisses became more fervent. Hair was pulled. Magee's knees and calves were up to Tony's chest. She was slamming her hips and buttocks against him with a ferocity he only now remembered. The thrusts were complete and violent.

Her vibrant exhaling became soft whimpers, full whimpers, low moans, and finally full-throated feral sounds begging for completion. As she approached nir-vana, she began to lick his upper torso from nipples to scalp, all the while trying to impale herself. It took every bit of strength for Tony not to be lost in the moment. The trembling foretold her release. So visceral, it was a re-lease of ten thousand years; so familiar, it was a release of his yesterdays; so exciting, it was a promise of future pleasure. Magee continued to pile drive and contract. To-ny joined her in paradise. His climax began where the scrotum and spinal column met, coursing up to his neck, arms, and legs, and finally nearly buckling his knees. They bounced like two marionettes. They did not fall.

The musk of love covered them, like a wet wool blanket.

"I have missed you, Anthony. I guess I never stopped loving you."

"Magee, I feared this would happen. Yet, I wanted it to happen. Now I don't know what to do. I care deeply about you. I always have. But I—we—need time to think through what has happened and what could happen. Will you give me time? How much, I don't know. But I do know I must reach a decision quickly or go insane."

"That's fair."

All the while they were talking, they were dressing. Like a husband and wife, who just took care of business and now must go to work. Was it lovers or just old friends who functioned that way?

Tony returned the file and adjusted the camera to its original position. The files for Road Developers were empty. Not even a paper clip was sliding on the bottom of the boxes. Someone was hiding something. Wilson and Weaver? Who else had motive and access? Only cops. The same cops who, when they observed the monitoring devices in the stacks, would know that Tony and Magee were aware of them. The hunters had become the rabbits, and the rabbits, the hunters.

CHAPTER 9

Sing Sing:

Eugene Eichelberger was killed in a brawl in the laundry a few years ago. It was listed as a race-related incident, and the old white guy was just in the wrong place at the wrong time. Got shanked by Hector Hernandez. Gene was the only one to be seriously hurt, and there was only one shank. All the others just got badly beaten. The brawl ended before the guards arrived. Gene was murdered, and the combatants just left the arena. What were they covering? Something was rotten on the Hudson. Hernandez was a lifer. Convicted of shooting two small-time dealers on the Lower East Side. Cash for Candy went bad. Hector was wounded, arrested, and given twenty-five to life for his good citizenship. Left a wife and two babies. For the incidental stabbing of Gene Eichelberger, Hector received solitary for five years and the full life term for his original offenses.

Tony headed up the various expressways to Ossining. Turning left at the station, he met the first of three gates: two for autos and one for people. He passed muster at each stop.

His appointment with Hector was for one p.m. Seated, he opened his folder with tablet and pen. This was a gift from Magee nearly eight years ago. It was beautiful. Moroccan leather, brass corners, and his initials in the lower right corner of the front. It even had pockets for his cards and small notes. Tony ran his hands over the hide and thought good thoughts.

The slamming of doors and the shuffling of the shackles broke Tony's reverie. The guard escorted the medium-sized, well-built Hispanic into the interrogation room. The orange jumpsuit was personalized with Hector's number—three-four-six-nine-five. He sat.

Tony waved at the guard. "Guard, we'll be okay. You can leave us alone. We just want to talk."

After attaching the hand and leg shackles to rings bolted to the floor and the metal table, the guard exited stage right. His part was complete.

"You got any smokes, man."

"Sorry, I quit years ago. Want some gum?"

Hector took the whole pack. The chain rattling through the floor ring made an ominous sound.

"Hector, I've come up here to learn why you killed Gene Eichelberger during the laundry room riot. Why him? What did he ever do to you?"

"He was nothing to me, man. Why do you want to know?"

"I think he was something to you. Was he your bitch? Or, someone who spurned you?"

"That old white dude was nobody's bitch. He was nothing to me."

"Then why did you kill him? I mean, with the Aryan Brotherhood in the room, you could have killed any one of them. Why Eichelberger? Did you do it because they wanted you to kill a Jew? Were you on the side of the Brotherhood and not Los Hermanos?"

"I am Hermanos forever. I hate the Brotherhood. I didn't know the old guy was a Kike until after I did him."

"Then why did you do it?"

"Why do you want to know this thing? What's it worth to you if I know something? I mean what's in it for me?"

"I want to know this thing because it may relate to a bigger investigation—one dealing with police corruption and murder sanctioned by the police. If what you tell me helps in this investigation, I might get the DA to reduce your punishment. Maybe not in years, but in confinement. If you don't tell me, I can get the DA to extend your solitary."

"Why should I tell you anything? I mean, you're just like all the rest of the cops. You want, want, want, and you don't give, give, give. I got my deal. It works. Now you want to change it. Fuck you."

"How about if I get you sent to North Dakota, where your wife and kids can never see you? How about I get you sent to an Ultra Max Solitary? You get to see the sunshine once a week. You have no communication, whatsoever with the outside. No visitors. No telephone. No letters. You're dead, but you don't die. Or, how about I make it easy for your wife and kids to visit every week. Get you conjugal visitation. Or, how about I get you and your family out of here. Out of the state. Witness protection?"

"Why would you do this for me, man?"

"I believe you know more about the killing of Gene Eichelberger than you have told anyone to date. I need that information for this special investigation. You could be a hero and be rewarded for your contribution, or you could be a real asshole and stay in this hell hole forever."

"I'm tired of talking about this, man. You bring me a deal from the DA, and I'll tell you anything you want to hear."

"If I bring a deal from the DA, you'll tell me the truth. If your story proves out, you could get out from under this rock. If your story falls on its ass, you will rot in solitary."

"Guard, I think we're done here."

Who is the fisherman? Who is the fish? Sometimes, if the fish is big enough, he gets the fisherman. It is past the time to cut bait. I have to go to the DA. Before that, should I go to Brainerd? Must not go around Brainerd's back or Uncle Jimmy could become vindictive. Is Brainerd a leak? Does he wear dirty linen like Wilson and Weaver? How much should I tell anybody? How much will Wilson and Weaver learn of my actions? Today?

From the DA? Will that knowledge get me killed?

Sharing his files with Franklin Ranck looks like the move of a genius. Before he talked to the DA or Brainerd, Tony had to gather all his facts and assumptions. This meant reviewing his files, tapes, and notes, sit with Franklin.

Franklin Ranck had been Tony's friend since before college. They drifted through the drug haze of years ago together. Tony went deeper into the pit while Franklin went to work as a legal suit. He left the corporate world of expensive clothing, lavish offices, and thin veneer long ago. His head left two years before his body walked through the oak doors. Now Franklin's clients were people who knew him before he wore a suit or had faced him in his legal life. People feared and loved his honesty. Everybody respected him for it, even those he had walked out on.

His job was to protect his clients. He did so with great vigor and strength of character. He was the best. To him the law was a game he must win every time he played. The bigger the prize, the harder he worked. Often his actions were considered vicious. But he was not without compassion. He would win. His favorite wall hanging was a lovely needlepoint sampler with flowers and butterflies given to him by his mother:

> *Yea, though I walk through*
> *the valley of the shadow of death,*
> *I will feel no evil,*
> *for I am the meanest son-of-a-bitch in the valley.*

His offices were down a long dimly lit marble hall in a building that was on someone's short list for demolition. He'd just find another out-of-the-way space. Tony knocked on the door. The ganja smell had seeped into the hall.

As the door opened, the heady aroma was powerful.

"Tony, it's good to see you. What can I do for three hundred dollars an hour?"

"Jesus, Franklin, must you always smoke that stuff?"

"Doing my best to fight glaucoma. When I was straight, I was fuzzy. When I went straighter, I was still fuzzy. It's nature's aromatherapy for human unreality. Want some?"

"Not now. We need to talk. I need your best counsel. Can you do that for me now?"

"Sounds like you're in deep shit."

"Not yet. But, I'm about to do the feces flop."

"Sit on the couch and put your feet up. Relax. Want some coffee or a soda? Got no booze. Quit that shit during the daylight hours."

"Nah, I'm fine. Before I tell you what I stepped in today. Have you kept the material I sent you?"

"You betcha'."

"Did you have a chance to review the items and their content?"

"As your friend and counselor, I examined the material. And, I gotta' tell ya', whatever you think, what you have stumbled onto is really big—either in your mind or in reality. I'm not sure which."

"Let me tell you what I learned and what I think I

learned today in the basement of One Police Plaza and at Ossining."

Tony laid out all the facts—everything—to the one person he could trust. Trust with his life. Magee was almost back on that very short list. She was a cop first, his lover second. After six hundred dollars' worth of time, the boys agreed to the appropriate next steps. They would meet with an assistant DA before seven a.m. tomorrow, lay out what Tony knew and suspected, secure the support of the DA's office, and get an assistant to go with them to Sing Sing. The faster they moved, the safer Tony would be. In this case, speed would not kill.

He called Connie, and they agreed to meet for dinner at nine at The East Sider, a chic bar near home. Tony headed back to the precinct to clear his desk. Email, voicemail, and snail mail brought him tons of information. But only a scant portion of it was useful. Delving into the police personnel file, Tony searched for information about Captain Patrick Lynch of the two-four. *Who was he? When did he die? How did he die? Suffolk County Police have the autopsy report.*

Tony's email asked for a copy. Probably tomorrow.

He had hoped dinner would be a respite. But Connie's incessant prattle about the overwhelming details pertinent to the expansion of The Seven Sisters shot that idea in the ass. It looked like they would be able to raise enough capital to set up an average of six franchises a month for eighteen months. Speed of expansion was the drug of success and excess. Real estate was the critical issue.

"Is it better to drop more franchises in fewer markets…say six or eight…than to spread out geographically and go where the space is less expensive, but immediate impact and ROI are limited? How will each unit be staffed? Who heads the unit? Who does the training? The first half-dozen units will be the most difficult to add from personnel and infrastructure standpoints. Tested systems must be in place before all this happens. Should equipment be purchased or leased? Who gives the best deal? On quantity and timeline. What area demographics offer the best-sustained membership growth? Not novelty visits. What are the traffic patterns near the real estate? Blah, blah, blah, blah, blah…"

She was like a child excruciatingly relating the details of her new portable dollhouse.

That night—hope, sleep…fitful sleep.

Assistant DA, George Marshall, was impressed, skeptical, and somewhat confused. His office never turned down a chance to lift a rock covering dirty cops. It must play hell with his conscience to work with and depend on a group then turn around and screw them over—if he had a conscience. Marshall's boss agreed that a trip to Ossining might well serve everyone's purposes. He gave Marshall the approval to negotiate for information. There was no time to call ahead for a reservation in the interrogation room. Before eight a.m. the three rushed to the unmarked police car and headed north. The irony of the mode of transportation was not lost on Tony.

Franklin, George, and Tony sat on one side of the table and awaited the arrival of the font of knowledge.

"Listen, you two. This is my show. I am the representative of the district attorney's office. I have the power to make the promise, which will extract the most information from this scum. Do not speak unless I request it. As of eight a.m., you are no more than passengers on my train."

Franklin arched an eyebrow. "On behalf of my client, fuck you, you pompous piece of putrid poop. We brought this career-maker to you, and we will lead the investigation until we're ready to turn it over to your boss, or you. Your choice. We can leave now, and you'll be left with a massive omelet on your suit. Or, we can stay and conduct our interview. Besides, if it succeeds, it's your success. If it fails, it's our fault. As of eight a.m., you are a plenipotentiary representing the throne. There are numerous things we did not divulge to either you or your boss. As we go forward in this investigation, we will use these facts to extract more information when we deem it appropriate. We can or cannot insert you and your power to increase or lighten Hector's load. So, sit there, listen, learn, and speak when spoken to."

The prisoner shuffled in, sat, and was locked down. The guard exited stage right.

"Hector, my name is Franklin Ranck. You've already met Detective Sattill. This other gentleman is George Marshall, an assistant DA in New York. Today we would like to discuss exactly why you killed Gene Eichelberger."

"Who the fuck are you, man? Why are you here?"

"Sorry, I am Detective Sattill's lawyer. I am not a

member of NYPD, the PBA, or the FOP. I am a private citizen. Would you like a cigarette?"

"Sure, thanks."

Hector kept the entire pack. Franklin pulled a second pack from his jacket pocket and placed it in front of his notepad.

Bait.

Hector took a long drag. "Okay, as I told the detective. Before I tell you anything, I want to know what I get out of the deal."

"Your reward for cooperation will be determined by Mr. Marshall at the end of our conversation. The more truth you tell, the greater will be your reward. And you won't have to wait for heaven. The truth will set you free of this place."

"How do I know this is straight up? I mean I've been fucked over by the cops before. Thought I made deals, only to find out later that what I thought I heard them say they did not say."

Franklin nodded to Marshall.

"Mr. Hernandez, my picture ID will assure you that we are serious about this Q and A session, because I am who I say I am. If I tell you something like you will be released from solitary, or you will be able to see your children twice a week, or you will have conjugal visits, you will get them in exchange for the truth about the murder of Gene Eichelberger. If you are not forthcoming, you will stay here doing whatever it is you do all day long. If you lie to us, you will be transferred far away. Say, North Dakota. Then, you may never see your family.

Minimum contact with anyone and maximum sensory deprivation for you. A hell of a way to die."

Hector looked at Tony and nodded recognition that the DA had repeated what Tony had told him the day before. The skeleton of the deal was on the table. Now, to put flesh on the bones.

"Before I tell you guys anything, you got to know I'm scared. If it ever gets out that I told you anything, I am dead, and my family is dead. My babies would get their throats slit, and my wife gang-raped before all her bones were broken. So, you got to guarantee my safety and my family's safety after today."

Franklin nodded to Marshall.

"Depending on what you tell us today, we are prepared to provide both you and your family protection immediately. Like in one hour."

"Okay."

"Hector, why did you kill Gene Eichelberger?"

"The man paid me. Really, he paid my family."

"Please explain. Who is the man?"

"There were two of them. Wilson and Weaver. They came to me. They were not in on my bust. You know the two mugs I capped. Wilson and Weaver did not arrest me, but they watched during the interrogation and trial, and they came to me two weeks after I got here. Eichelberger was already here. They said they would take care of my wife and babies if I took care of the old Jew. The two cops promised to give my wife two grand a month for as long as I kept my mouth shut after I wasted Eichelberger. The cops never told me why they wanted the old guy capped. They just did. I had them make two payments before the riot was staged. I thought they were for real, so I did my part. Since then, they have been steady with the cash to my family."

The gravity and enormity of the event hit Tony's gut. Wilson killed his stepfather, the man who cut the cop great deals, the man who was the fall guy for the bank. Franklin's voice seemed so far away.

"How can we confirm this transaction? How do we know you're not pulling our chains?"

"Get in touch with my wife. You know where she lives. She'll confirm everything. I told her everything about my deal and what to do with the money. Each month she gets the cash, she puts five hundred dollars into two savings accounts: one for her and one for my babies. She lives off the rest and what she makes at the bodega. You can check her bank records. I told her not to be splashy with the bread. She is a good woman. She even gives a little to her folks and my folks. It's like I'm still working and takin' care of my family. Now what do I get?"

"You mean that's all."

Marshall was upset with the simplicity of the truth.

"That's all I know. I don't know why they wanted the old guy capped. I never asked."

Franklin continued to exert his control over the situation and George Marshall. "George, I think you should call your boss and tell him what you just extracted from Mr. Hernandez. I think you and your boss would be well served to extricate Mr. Hernandez from this luxurious spa. I think your boss would be well served to find Mrs. Hernandez and her children and escort them into the waiting arms of Mr. Hernandez. The four of them should stay hidden from everyone, including Detective Sattill and me, for a few days or weeks so that this entire mess can be placed at the proper door. We still have much to do. Now, please do your duty."

Assistant DA Marshall used his special cell phone—he had three. To call his boss's special phone required that Marshall use his. Franklin disdainfully eyed Marshall. No one was that important.

"Our office is sending a van to pick-up Mr. Hernandez. His family will be in route to see him within twenty minutes. They will be united and hidden within the hour. Our office is processing the paperwork for a transfer that will deposit him in another prison. Except he will not be there physically. Mr. Hernandez will simply be a phantom prisoner in another prison. But I will know where he is. His family will live outside the prison in a nice townhouse for now. We will repeat the questioning and take statements—hard copy and video. Thank you, gentlemen, you have been of great assistance."

"George, we're going to wait for the van and see you on your merry way."

As promised, the entire extrication took one hour. As the van headed off to the unknown, Tony and Franklin looked blankly at each other.

"So, what did we learn?"

"A great deal, Tony. But just the first nail in the coffin. Now we have to work fast and smart to put a lot of bodies in the coffin before it is sealed. We have to stay three steps in front of the DA as his bureaucratic schlock troops. We have to stay ahead of the information leaks. The faster we move; the more glory will be ours. God, it's good to be back in battle. Conflict is such a rush. Now, we need some extra hands. Who do you trust?"

"Detective Margaret Myers." Tony blurted out Magee's name without thinking. Maybe his gut was telling him what his mind did not want to deal with. Regardless, he could not erase the tape.

"Wasn't she your lover in blue? Isn't she married now?"

"Yes, and no. She's divorced. Besides, I've told her nearly everything, and I know she wants to help. For me. For her promotion. For the force."

"I'll call her. You talk to her. Tell her what we must do."

That completed, Tony asked to use Franklin's cell to call Connie.

"Hey, C, listen. This case and Brainerd's demands are making me crazy. I have to work this weekend to get everyone off my back. If you want to go to the beach, please do so, but I've got to stay in the city."

"Tony, what wonderful timing. I have been wrestling with telling you that I have to cloister with the financial and business teams down amongst the towers of Wall Street. So I can't go to the beach this weekend either. Maybe between our jobs, we can find time to have a nude dinner at home or catch a movie. Anyway, one weekend in the city won't kill either one of us. Love ya, sweetie. See you tonight. I'll be late."

After Tony hung up, Franklin shook his head. "Tony, your sex life is none of my business, but your safety is. So, you got to be really careful with two women. One of your heads knows the truth. The other knows nothing but pleasure."

The two headed back to the city and Magee's apartment—a safe house, no eyes and ears of the law.

Tony made the introductions. "Margaret Ann Myers. This is Franklin Fontain Ranck. Franklin, this is Margaret."

"Please call me Magee. Tony does, and it makes me feel comfortable. Have we met before?"

"Yes, a number of years ago, when the three of us did strange pharmaceutical things to our bodies. A party at a penthouse on Central Park West. Christmas, I think. You wore a very short green dress that was open from neck to navel."

"Well, that's a little more than I remember. But I'll take your word for it."

"Magee, from your home laptop, can you access files from the NYPD system?" Franklin asked.

"Yes, I can access anyone's files if I know their two passwords."

"Okay, you two check and see if there is anything of importance recently sent to your workstation. Tony, check yours. While you're about it, check your respective voicemails."

Nothing of importance was in Magee's two emails.

Tony had received a message from Kelly and Echlebaum. They were demanding a meeting on Saturday at eight a.m. at the precinct. The invitation could not be ignored. Also, the Suffolk County Coroner's report on the death of Captain Patrick Lynch was in. Lynch appeared to have drowned in his own blood and the water from Long Island Sound in some form of a boating accident over the Memorial Day weekend. There was one trauma to the back of the head. Blunt trauma. Indications were that the victim ingested some blood before falling into the water. Blood/alcohol level indicated the victim was drunk when he took the dive. Some nibbling of the flesh on the fingers, arms, and legs was caused by fish in the sound. A small puncture wound on the right side of the neck appeared to have caused the artery to bleed into the stomach and lungs.

"Holy shit. Franklin, Magee. Look at this. It looks like our Handyman has been busy before the recent rash. Is it coincidence or connected? The bump on the head is the obvious difference. But the date rape drug was not on the street then. Shit, if we can't connect Charlotte and Chakika, how the hell are we going to connect them with Lynch?"

Franklin jumped to the lead. Orders were barked, furniture was moved, and pictures were removed from the long wall in the living room. He was bouncing around like a drop of water on a white-hot skillet. The working frenzy had commenced.

"Magee, do you have any grocery bags and markers or crayons?"

"Yes, why?"

"In my foggy history, we used to put keywords, phrases, and people on the wallboard to see if there were any way we could connect them or what their significance was in the grand scheme of things. Let's get going. Magee, tear open the bags and flatten them. Do you have push pins, so we can mount the paper on a wall? Tony, get my case, it's got the file. Do you have a micro-recorder, Magee? Play the interview with Elija. Review the all the tapes. Put all the names on one bag, places on another, and dates on a third. I have to step out for a moment, but we can start when I return. Go. Go. Go. Get to work."

The rush was nearly palpable. Franklin slid through the front door. His cohorts' activity became intense. The effect of adrenaline was obvious. All the fatigue of the day was gone. The thrill of exploration swept away all the anxiety of the project. Where and why had Franklin gone?

Tony moved to a window and spotted Franklin as he turned the corner. Tony ran to the patio on back of the apartment to no avail. Without X-ray vision, Tony couldn't see Franklin through the walls of other buildings.

Why the departure? Why the promise of a quick return? Weed?

"Magee, I'll bet you a hundred kisses and two hundred thigh licks that Franklin will smell of hoo-hah when he returns."

"You're on. Here they are: twelve of Gristede's best.

Gutted wide, flattened, and push-pinned to the wall. Ready for your part."

The door reopened, and Franklin entered. His countenance had changed. He was calmer. "All set you two?"

The odor was unmistakable.

"We are. Magee, you owe me."

"A debt I relish paying."

"Franklin, why the toking?"

"It helps me think. After smoking, I can take mental excursions that would have not been possible, were I straight. I can look at details and see many big pictures. I can see big pictures and notice the detail that's out of place. Okay?"

"Okay."

"And I was frightened. This is the first big case I have been involved in since I left the shirts to become a skin. The rush is fantastic. It's like speed. But I'm not sure I can handle the pressure again, and I don't want to let you two down. Consider my toking to be a morale-boosting exercise. A rounding and smoothing of the edges. Okay?"

The time-consuming labor began. The puzzle was vast and time was not a vast commodity. Whatever the three were to find must be found immediately at the latest. The element of surprise, if it existed, could not be lost. There were many missing pieces: some small and other huge. Connections were key. There were obvious connections. Most of them legal and non-threatening. But the underlying connections, the ones that drove, twisted, and perverted, were hidden. These must be discovered and uncovered. Obviously, the First Bank and Road Developers were in lockstep. Benedetto, Gentile, Eichelberger—and stepson Wilson, Weaver—both father and son, Mirtan, Alphonse, Alphonse Jr., Carole—Carol or Chakika. How could the illegal connections be proven? How could bank and corporate records be accessed and analyzed? This would require instant help from the DA or the feds. Franklin grabbed his cell phone, dialed, and asked for Assistant DA Marshall. He was told to leave a message, and the operator would have the assistant DA call back. That took an agonizing five minutes. Franklin scribbled the caller ID notation on his pad. He would not wait again.

"While you guys have been vacationing upstate, Detective Sattill and I have been scouring the details of this morass-like maze. A critical first step is to clearly define, with facts, figures, dates, and names the relationship between First Bank and Road Developers. We need you to get search and seizure warrants executed pre-dawn Monday. Will you do it?"

"I'll have to see."

Franklin frowned at the tepid response. "Jesus, man, the three of us are deep in this shit and asking you for help. Help, I might add, which can only benefit the careers of certain public officials. We can come to your office tonight and layout the details of what we know. You can then go to the judge and get the warrants on Sunday. Yes, we'll stay out of your activity, so you can get the good ink. A little quid pro quo, my friend."

"Ten. See you then."

Franklin put the phone back in his pocket and turned to Magee. "Magee, if you want to come along and extend your exposure, you are more than welcome. If you choose not to join our Friday night soiree, I understand."

"I'm there. I go wherever Tony goes. Besides, if I don't go, you two would have to kill me."

Franklin nodded. "Permit me to posit a query. Who can we honestly eliminate from the list of people on our wall of shame?"

Tony shrugged. "Well, I heard last week that JJ Rierdan took early retirement for family reasons. His wife has advanced MS. He wants to spend time with her and their children. He, Elija, and I were in line for the next step up. So, he's out. Besides, his name has not surfaced in any area of our interest. One of Elija's state police handlers, Byers, has faded into Alzheimer's land. Another handler died. Rissi just got dead. Wallace of the *Post* is alive and has tried to get involved in the murders to further his career. But he has not shown his face in the nefarious deeds of the bank and builder."

Franklin snapped his fingers. "Bingo. Wallace is perfect. Let us put his ambition and greed to work for us. How can we use the power of the press to our advantage?"

Magee rubbed her chin. "We could leak elements of our investigation to the newspaper. The factoids get printed after the DA has secured the files—the evidence. And those who thought they were protected by layers of near anonymity begin to panic. Panicky people do dumb things. This plan is given to the DA's office before execution, so that they can keep a close eye on the dumb activities of the exposed. When the exposed go running to their handlers, the DA can move up the crime chain. All this without having to give walks to the lower echelon. It's like that old game at Halloween where you put a lot of dog shit in a paper bag, place the bag at the front door, and set the bag on fire. Then you ring the doorbell and hide behind a tree to watch the guy stomp the bag to put out the fire and get shit all over his shoes. He would never have stepped on the bag, were it not on fire. His logic is diverted by the crisis of the moment. Pure panic reaction. We will make the bad guys the precipitators in their own demise. We do the work, and the DA gets the credit."

Tony hugged her. "Magee, you are a devious, evil, manipulative bitch. The plan is pure genius. Better than anything I could have dreamed up. Much more Machiavellian."

The newspaper paged Dick Wallace. He called the paper. The paper gave him Franklin's cell number. Wallace called Franklin.

"Mr. Wallace, thanks for calling. I am here with Detective Sattill. You two have met previously. He has some information you might find interesting, about nefarious deeds and police corruption worthy of an article on page three. Would you be interested in talking to us?"

"Who are you?

"Sorry, my name is Franklin F. Ranck, Esquire. Call me Franklin. I am Detective Sattill's personal legal counsel. Can you meet with us around midnight?"

"I suppose."

"Good. Where would you like to meet?"

"How about my place?"

"Great, Your place it is, Mr. Wallace. See you after twelve."

Click.

Franklin grinned. "That will give us time to get our leaked facts straight and confirm our plan with the DA, as well as give our ferret a chance to bug the interview room. Now, what do we want to leak?"

CHAPTER 10

12 Center Street:

The doorway to the Municipal Building was guarded by cops and electronics. The desk in the rotunda was solid oak and very ornate. Rumor had it that it is a full-scale replica of the Information Desk in Grand Central Station. It was not. One call to the DA's office was the visa to the place of power. Off the elevator, the sounds of six shoes, the strikes of six heels, and the *flumps* of six soles were not just loud—they also reverberated off the hallway walls and the fourteen-foot ceilings. The building's marble was not so much worn as it had a rich patina. Dirt and oils rubbed by millions of shoes over five decades. The weekly washing and waxing had accentuated the paths of people seeking help in their quest for justice. Lights glowed beyond the reception area at one end of the hall. The contrast between the hard noise of the footsteps and the warmth of the light was intriguing to Tony.

Marshall stuck out his hand. "Well, Mr. Ranck and Detective Sattill. And…I don't believe we've met, Miss…"

"I am Detective Margaret Myers, Shield Number five, six, two, one. Assigned to the two-seven, under the command of Captain Elliot."

"Thank you, Detective Myers. Exactly what is your connection to this evening's festivities?"

"Detective Sattill came to me the other day, and we discussed, on a professional basis, what he has uncovered, learned, and surmised. I have assisted Detective Sattill in the past. He felt confident that I would give him sound counsel, like the counsel he has received from Mr. Ranck. The three of us have reviewed extensive matter pertinent to an investigation into the alleged illegal activities of Road Developers and the First Bank of Long Island. We have reached the conclusions you will hear tonight. Detective Sattill and I felt that two police officers, who trust each other, would be a substantial supplemental force to your investigation."

"Yes, thank you, Detective Myers. So professional. So rehearsed. Shall we adjourn to the conference room?"

"Marshall, is that the one you guys have bugged?" Franklin asked.

"Not tonight."

"Well, just in case you forgot to turn off the recording devices, tonight let us just sit in the reception area and discuss what we think should be done. Please call your boss."

"District Attorney Price is not here yet. But he will be so shortly."

"Then we'll wait here, if you don't mind."

Franklin had a way of maneuvering people and discussions so that the other party was never in control. His maneuvering was on the long end of snotty. He knew it, and so did they. Ten minutes and DA Price came down the hall.

"Shall we adjourn to the conference room?"

Franklin shook his head. "We shall meet right here, thank you. Let us lay out what we have learned since our last visit, what we think should be done, and what we are going to do."

The plan discussion bubbled with reasonable give and take. Price and Marshall wanted hard information and data before they went to a judge on a Sunday. Judges did not like to be interrupted on a day away from the bench. Franklin agreed to provide tapes. If the information was credible, they saw no problem with securing a warrant for the pre-dawn Monday raids. Magee and Tony laid out her proposal for leaking information. They touched on what information would be given to Wallace after *The Midnight Hour*. An agreement was reached.

Wallace's neighborhood would never be confused with that of Mr. Rogers. Despite the very recent incursion of the yuppies, Tenth Avenue was a war zone. The Westies, Banditos, and Uhurus jostled for shrinking territorial power. There were never any murders, just disappearances. As the ranks of one faction were culled, the other two preyed on it. Then each other. This cycle had been spinning for three decades. Only the people suffered. But they did so in silence. Wallace's building was "remodeled" within the past decade. Yellow firebrick and aluminum entrance accouterments attested to the fashion sense of the owner. A note on the buzzer panel read…

Mr. Ranck, meet me at O'Bryans.

Just another dirty bar in a dirty neighborhood. Wallace was in a side booth facing the door. He acknowledged Sattill. Introductions and IDs were passed around. Wallace wiggled, as if to adjust a mic. Now he leaned forward, ostensibly to keep the conversation at a whisper. This was another ploy to ensure effective recording. The information began to drip then trickle, like water from an old tap. Great care was needed to not give the messenger too much information—yet. Give him a taste for now— enough to stimulate his interest in a story that would make his career. Numerous related innuendoes. First Bank, Road Developers, Benedetto, Eichelberger. Greed drove both the protagonists and the journalist. Wallace feverishly scribbled notes. He probed for very specific dates and transactions but was steered away from too much truth.

"Now, here is the next step, Mr. Wallace. We will meet with you at District Attorney Marshall's office at Twelve Center Street Sunday at noon. That will give you time to corroborate some of this information. At that time, we will be in a position to divulge much more of the case. The DA will also be in a position to answer your questions. You can break the story on Monday. Okay?"

"Yeah, sure."

"Then it's set, we'll meet on Sunday."

On the way home, Tony checked his voicemail. Connie, calling at eleven-thirty, missed him. He arrived home at one-thirty. Connie was fast asleep on the couch. As he searched for a blanket to cover her and removed the small tray of partially eaten food, he heard the music and voice-over from the TV. On the big screen was a loop of rough-cuts of an infomercial and two thirty-second commercials about The Seven Sisters. The expansion was beginning to go public. Slumber was his couch companion. Before Tony's eyes were completely shut, the alarm sounded. He couldn't be late for the latest installment of the Kelly-Echlebaum witch-hunt.

The precinct's crew was always lighter on weekends than on weekdays. Crime went up on weekends, but protection went down. Always few regulars plus guys suckin' up the OT to make the boat payment or college tuition for the kid. Captain Brainerd was in his office awaiting Mutt and Jeff. He waved to Tony.

"Ya' know, laddy, ya' never got me that report on yer pal Washington. The heat will git pretty intense in a few days, and I need to know what you have uncovered. I've cut you enough slack, fer dis reason or dat. But now I gotta' to know. The deadline is Tuesday, first ting. Well, I see our friends are here. Come in, gentlemen. How can we help you?"

"You can't help us at all, Captain. But detective Sattill can help himself if he comes clean, as it were."

Kelly grinned at Echlebaum. "Detective Sattill, we have irrefutable evidence that directly ties you to the murders of Charlotte Jenks and Chakika Washington. We need you to enlighten us as to a few other details of your involvement. So let us adjourn to an interview room."

"We'd be glad to assist you in your investigation."

"This has nothing to do with you, Captain. You are not invited to our tea party. You are not permitted to observe or record our conversation in any manner. So please remain here or go home, while we interrogate the suspect."

The old man was crestfallen. He couldn't protect or help his nephew. He couldn't facilitate the investigation. He couldn't benefit from the findings. He had been used and cut out of the loop by the experts. Maybe Brainerd was trying to do Tony a solid all along. Help Tony's career by letting him climb over a competitor. Uncle Jimmy was not part of the inner circle. He was just a bit player in this hugely confusing opus.

Somehow, Tony was relieved. "I need to call my PBA rep."

Kelly's grin was ominous. "That won't be necessary. This isn't a real interrogation. It's more like a discussion between cops and a person of interest. We just want to tie up loose ends. Okay?"

From his new perspective as a suspect, Tony saw the peeling, drab green paint on the walls of the interview room. Bits and pieces of refuse. Dirt in the corners. The cigarette and sweat had created an air pollution that had glazed the see-through mirror and the windows—one in the door and one to the airshaft. The reek of fear and fail-ure hung in the air. The dank stench collected over the years was now stuffed up his nose. The fluorescent tubes flickered randomly. This caused eyes to flutter impercep-tibly. After a half-hour, this, in turn, produced disorienta-tion in the interviewee. Precinct purgatory.

Kelly and Echlebaum attacked from both sides. A barrage of questions from alternating sources. Kelly's voice was raised and staccato. Echlebaum intones each probe. Questions were always within each other, like the little Russian doll toys. The outside question could not be answered without first understanding the inside ques-tions. Then none could be answered alone. The answers could or could not apply to all. And it began. One ques-tion on top of another. The sources were different.

"We will be brief, if you cooperate, or very long if you stonewall us," Kelly said. "As I said before, our evi-dence is irrefutable, but we have a few questions. Why would you want to kill Ms. Jenks and Mrs. Washington? Can you provide proof as to your whereabouts on the days preceding the murders? Were you having affairs with both women? Did you hate their partners so much that you killed the women?"

"Why did you do it?" Echelbaum asked.

"I didn't kill either or both women."

"The evidence says you are the man. When, before you killed her, did you last sleep with Ms. Jenks? When did you last fuck Mrs. Washington?"

"My relationship with both women was purely so-cial."

"Bullshit, you shared a summer house with Ms. Jenks. We know what goes on in the beach houses. Drugs and lots of group sex. Did she spurn you? Was she into kinky group sex? Did your version of one-on-one sex get out of control?"

"There was no relationship between me and Charlotte, other than that we were members of the same group who shared a summer house. There was never any physical congress between us."

"Were you pissed that she was fucking somebody else who made her HIV positive? Are you HIV positive? We can help you if you are. Were you afraid of contracting the disease? Did her boyfriend, Bill Davis, contract the disease? Have you been tested? Whose baby was she carrying? We could test you for the death disease."

"I did not know she was HIV positive until I received the report from the coroner's office, just like you guys. I never slept with Charlotte Jenks. And you'll never get my blood without a court order. Which you don't have or we wouldn't be having this discussion."

"We know you were investigating Detective Washington to uncover dirt about him. Discredit him so you would be the only one available—notice I did not say suitable—to head-up CAT. Why would you compromise his wife? Or did she offer herself to protect her husband from your investigation? Did the sex get out of hand like with Ms. Jenks?"

"I never had sex with Mrs. Washington. Hell, I only saw her two times a year."

"Do you like fucking niggers? Did she moan good?

Did you get your jollies watchin' the black ass bounce up and down? Did she give better head than Ms. Jenks?"

"Move on, guys. You're getting nowhere with this inquisition. And your stupidity is beginning to aggravate me."

"Where did you learn to kill like that? Do you use an ice pick or a special weapon? Did you read about the method in a *Soldier of Fortune Magazine* or some old police file? How did you learn the proper angle of insertion?"

"First, I did not kill the women. Second, I have no idea what weapon was used. Third, I have never read *Soldier of Fortune* or any similar magazine. Fourth, I have no idea as to the angle of insertion."

"Where did you get the date-rape drug?"

"I have never been in possession of this date-rape drug to which you refer. I had nothing to do with their murders, goddammit."

"We've checked on your alleged alibis for the twenty-four hours preceding the two murders. There are a few very big-time gaps. Why don't you tell us what you were doing the day before you were called to each crime scene?"

"I can't recall which days are in question."

"Sure, you can, Detective. Just think about it. The day before your pussy squad was called to each of your murders. I'll bet you have a real good alibi for each day."

"The day before we were called to Charlotte Jenks's home, I was out of the station house. I had to run to the office of records, I went to the public library to do research, and I went to the gym to work out. The day before we were called to Mrs. Washington's home I was at the precinct."

"What were you doing during the evenings?"

"After dinner, I went home to bed."

"With whom did you have dinner on both nights? We'd like to verify your menus."

"Ms. Connie Wilhaus before the Jenks case was opened, and Detective Myers of the two-seven before the Washington case was opened."

"Where can we contact Ms. Connie Wilhaus?"

"She is my lover. You can call her at my apartment. I am sure you'll recognize her voice from the bugs you planted in my place."

They never blinked. Nary a twitch.

"What is Detective Myers's first name?"

"Margaret."

"God, you Italians have *waaaay toooo* much testosterone. You fuck everybody. Do you plan to kill Ms. Wilhaus and Detective Myers the same way you killed the other women?"

"That's enough. I've had it. I'm getting out of this chair and exiting the room and the building unless you arrest me. And, if you want to arrest me, I'll call my PBA rep and the lawyer from the PBA. Then it will get really ugly. Soooooo, bye-bye, guys."

"Sit down, asshole. You'll leave when we are through with you. Not before."

Tony began to rise, Kelly moved to put his hand on Tony's shoulder.

"If you touch me, you rotten fuck, I'll drop you where you stand. Then I'll shove the leg of this chair up your ass. This is my house. You are an uninvited guest."

Captain Brainerd's entrance was like a bucket of cold water dumped on angry dogs. Silence and stares all around. His demeanor screamed authority.

"Tony, let's grab lunch. Sorry I can't invite you boys, but my budget is tight."

Brainerd wrapped his arm around Tony's shoulders. The uncle escorted the interviewee to the safety of the captain's office. The skunks skulked from the precinct.

"That's a big one you owe me, laddy. Now let us enjoy a sandwich and a couple of cold ones at McAn's over on Fourth. And, yes it's my treat."

Lunch at McAn's, beer and pastrami.

"You gotta' watch yer ass, boy. Those galoots like to play rough, and they got the brass on their side. They're worse than a coyote in search of meat or a young buck lookin' for pussy. They are relentless."

"Did you tell them about my investigation into the world of Elija?"

"Now, why would I do that? I'm tryin' to protect my ass and yer ass from the likes of them."

Tony knew the truth before he asked the question. The old man was playing like a big-league politician at the double-A level. He would lie to cover his activities and lie about the lie. For sure, Brainerd was another one not to be trusted. He was not a bumbling fool, he just meddled too much. The good feeling was replaced by the shadowy one. Uncle Jimmy just joined the ranks of Tony's interrogators, Wilson, and Weaver. Now Tony had to watch all sides of the fort. The bad guys had him surrounded.

Fuck, he almost forgot his one p.m. meeting in the DA's office. Scarfing the sandwich, he gulped the beer. "Gotta run."

"Where are you off to in such a hurry?"

"I forgot the errands I had to run before noon. Now I'm late. Thanks for the support and the lunch. See you on Monday."

"Don't forget you owe me the damned report by Tuesday."

Center Street—the brightness of the day eliminated all of last night's comfortable nooks and crannies from the halls. The patina of the marble floor was gone, replaced by light kicks. The solid, almost metallic, heel clicks were audible. The double doors to the DA's office were open. Tony could hear Franklin's wisecracks.

"Sorry I'm late. Let us begin."

Marshall nodded. "Before we turn over our complete files, including tapes and notes, I'd like to read the following: 'Detective Anthony William Sattill Jr., New York Police Shield number four, eight, six, three; Detective Margaret Ann Myers, New York Police Shield number five, six, two, one ; and John Franklin Fontain Ranck, Attorney at Law, are willingly cooperating with the office of the district attorney in its investigation of alleged crimes committed by Road Developers, Incorporated, and First Bank of Long Island. The three aforementioned are presenting material to the New York

District Attorney's Office to facilitate said investigation. To wit, flash drive files created by Detective Sattill, a tape of Detective Sattill's conversation with Detective Elija Washington New York Police Shield number four, nine, eight, seven, and the notes of all the conversations among the three aforementioned individuals. This information provided today is done so free of coercion or the promise of favorable status.' Now if you would sign and date this memo, as we do, you can have the material."

Signatures all around.

"Mr. Ranck, we will get back to you and the detectives if we find that this material is sufficient support for the warrants. We should schedule another meeting later today to discuss what we have reviewed and to ask any questions. It's now two o'clock. Let us plan to meet back here at nine tonight. We have a staff waiting to tear into this information. So, if you'll excuse us…"

"See you at nine."

"Guys, I've got some very mundane household errands to run, so I'll see you this evening," Magee said before she rushed off.

Tony sighed. "Franklin, I need a break. I got an ass kicking this morning from Kelly and Echlebaum."

"Whoa, tell me what that's all about."

"Man, I'm wiped. Okay, come up to my place. Connie's gone to work, so we can talk freely."

The subway was the fastest mode of transportation from one end of the island to the other, and it was the least expensive. As they entered Tony's place, he remembered that his secure domicile was not secure. He wrote Franklin a note to that effect. They grabbed a cooler of beer and an old beach blanket and headed for the park to stretch out under the trees, sip a few frosties, and solve the problems of the world. Maybe doze off for an hour. Tony had forgotten how much he envied Franklin's free-and-easy lifestyle. The non-work hours. The casual clothes. The anxiety-dispersing drugs. The grass was always greener in the other guy's stash. And it smoked better, too.

Franklin settled in. He had a relaxing stick already rolled. It was lighted, and they both got lit. The words tumbled from Tony's lips. He cross-referenced facts, and events to develop tangent theories. Franklin listened and occasionally acknowledged the viability of the theoretical connections. Tony tried to relate all the details of the interrogation, but he became confused as to which questions were asked when. He was not sure if he could remember all the questions. After about forty-five minutes of intense brain digging, the two had nodded off. Kids played nearby. Dogs romped around the blanket. The afternoon drifted.

Franklin sat upright. "The two cops said they had irrefutable evidence that linked you to the murders. Your fingerprints? Your semen? What else could it be?"

Tony was groggy. The drug experience was unusual. "What are you saying? It can't be my semen."

"Why?"

"The ME said the tails were broken as if the soldiers had been stored before being dumped. I love trophies of all kinds, but not that kind."

"They are claiming that something of you was found at both crime scenes. Either you left it there, or someone planted it. These can be the only two delivery modes, if you will. Your CAT squad claimed to have found no fingerprints because maybe they did not look in the right spots, because you told them where to look. Or, maybe your fingerprints were placed at the crime scene after the CAT squad left. What about the spit? The two ferrets would have to have some part of your body—saliva, fingernail, hair, blood—to run a DNA test. Then they would have to match the test results against the test of the semen found at both crime scenes. But that doesn't explain the cigarette butts. They could create a false match. They could send one set of material twice, claim it was different material found at different places, get the same results from two tests, and produce a match. So, if they got a piece of you, they use that as their base material. Then they claim the results of the DNA test were based on semen found at the scenes and your hair or whatever. Finally, the semen is 'lost' so it can never be rechecked. I mean the police are not above planting evidence. Or disposing of evidence that does not fit their theory. This assumes that it is not your semen at the scenes. But if it is, how did it get there, assuming you are innocent?"

"Fuck you. I'm innocent, and I'm confused. Either you're not being clear, or you have fogged my mind with the weed of crime."

"Easy, Tony, I'm just speculating. What part of your body could they have?"

"Not my blood. Not my fingernails. My coffee cup is

missing. Could they have gotten anything from that?"

"What was the state of the cup the last time you saw it?"

"Loaded with two weeks of dried coffee, cream, and sugar scum."

"The absence of recent saliva coupled with the coffee and the additives would make a DNA profile nearly impossible. But it could be enough for them to begin a witch-hunt. If I had to make a guess with your life, I'd guess that someone planted your fingerprints after you were there. Now the ferrets have to smooth out all the other wrinkles so that the prints don't come into question. They also have to be able to substantiate where they found the prints. The CAT squad, under your command and direction, must not have examined the places where the prints could have been found. Also, the placement of the prints has to be consistent with the murderer being at the scene. In other words, prints on the underside of the bathroom wastepaper basket don't cut it. The sooner we know what they have the faster we can short-circuit their case."

"Would you mind not presupposing my guilt?"

The two went back to Tony's and dropped off the park supplies. Tony wanted to shower. He was frightened. The hunter-turned-rabbit was in trouble.

Franklin searched Tony's CD collection, found two from The Stones. First up, "Sympathy for the Devil," "Under My Thumb," and "Paint it Black"—grand conspiracy, S and M, and drug-driven depression. Great emotions for the listener cops. He set the volume level at eighteen. Enough to mask any conversation or footsteps. The search for the bugs began. His guess was that there was one in each room and one on the phone. Pictures were shifted, furniture was moved, and ledges fingered. The one in the kitchen was easily found. One was under the bed. Nosiness knew no modesty. The dining area ceiling lamp was bare. But the Oriental rug was not. By standing in the middle of the living room, he determined the farthest corner. Somewhere in the corner and directed out to the center of the room would be the bug. The bottom shelf of the bookcase gave up its booty.

Tony silently reappeared from the bathroom and Franklin handed him the audio intruders—all crushed.

"How the hell did you find them? I mean, I knew they were here. How did you know where to look?"

"Corporate espionage is no different than police work. I've had bugs planted in boardrooms and lavatories. I just remembered the drill."

"Franklin, I left them alone because I didn't want them to know that I knew. If they knew that I knew, they would only increase their surveillance. I just avoided any discussions about my work. I was feeling like a prisoner in my own home. You have returned freedom of speech to me. A modern-day founding father."

"You acted as if you were a frightened rabbit. You should have behaved as if you were a hunter. Let the bastards know that you know. Knock them off guard. If you had become aggressive and not remained passive, you would have forced them to change their plan to something less than ideal. The change and the secondary plan would have put them at a disadvantage. Hold on to these, they might prove to be useful in an invasion of privacy suit. Now let's grab some dinner before our next stint with the DA. Melons or someplace nearer Center Street?"

"Downtown. One of those celebrity watering holes. You must know a bunch of them."

The beer and starlet-wannabe leering more than compensated for the mediocre food. They decided to walk to Center Street and arrived fifteen minutes early. Magee was behind them by five. The warmth, color, and comfort in the building was back. The conference room was a mess. Stacks of papers on the big table, side tables, and floor appeared to be categorized by subject. People entered with copies of documents and distributed paper to various stacks. The cross-referencing was daunting. Tony walked around the room and noted that some stacks were by name. Other stacks were by date. Others, on the big conference table, were under the headings of RD and FB. They seemed to form a pyramid. Each layer was titled. Tony saw a file, which was supposedly in one of the boxes he and Magee examined. Were the other missing files here? Were the missing pages to be found in this room?

Franklin noticed papers that were not provided by them. He pointed to this stack and winked at Tony and Magee. Obviously, the contributions of Tony, Magee, and Franklin had augmented the DA's collection. The case had started before Tony did. "Well, Mr. Marshall, your minions have been hard at work."

"And we're not done yet. I'm guessing we have a few more hours until we can properly prepare our request for the warrants. But, Mr. Ranck, Detective Sattill, and Detective Myers, as you can see, the combined total of all our resources will make the request a slam-dunk. If I can presuppose, I'd like to shake your hands. And, if District Attorney Price were here, he would like to shake your hands, too. Tonight, I am paying my last dues. Now, we should discuss what we will tell Mr. Wallace."

It was agreed that any conversation with Wallace should avoid the Handyman Murders and deal exclusively with the corruption investigation and police involvement in it and its cover-up. Tony tried to stay up until Connie came home, but to no avail.

The morning was different. Lovemaking was a basic need from both sides of the bed. Release from the stress of the days. Comfort in the arms of someone, who needed comfort.

CHAPTER 11

Bleeker Street:

Wallace was waiting for Tony, et al., in the rotunda of the Municipal Building. He looked like shit. Grimy clothes, beard stubble, matted hair—his costume *du jour,* every *jour.* "It's about time you guys showed."

Tony took the lead. "Sorry for the delay but the trains just don't run when we want them to. Shall we go to the DA's office?"

Franklin made the introductions. "Assistant DA Marshall, this is Mr. Richard Wallace of the *Post*. He is here at our suggestion. I have told him that you are in the position to discuss certain newsworthy elements of your ongoing investigation. So, this is your meeting."

"Mr. Wallace, thank you from coming to my office

on a Sunday. What I am about to tell you, we hope you will find sufficient for an article in your newspaper, but not until the final Morning Edition on Monday. If you agree, we will give you an exclusive. If you don't agree to our stipulations, you can read the story in the other papers."

"That seems simple enough. Tell me, why me?"

"You have expressed interest at other times in other and separate areas of our work. We feel we can trust you to provide accurate, objective reporting on this matter."

Marshall was an almost believable liar, and Wallace was unbelievably gullible and greedy. "Okay, yeah. Let's begin."

The spider spun his web: strands of fact, truth, hint, innuendo, and omission. The fly's eyes glistened with anticipation—fame, a by-line, and money. The hard facts were out in the open. The bad guys—Wilson, Weaver, Benedetto, Gentile—would be able to hide no longer. Some not-so-bad guys: Washington and Mirtan would suffer, too.

Wallace asked the anticipated questions. Nothing out of the ordinary. He wanted to know the involvement of the lawyer and two detectives. Marshall did a good dance around the question, implying that the three were working for the DA's office. Franklin had an awareness of the banking laws and procedures and specific corporate knowledge about Road Developers. The two from the police force were not informants. Blah, blah, blah…

"How is this investigation tied to the Handyman Murders?"

"It is not in any way tied to the murders of Ms. Charlotte Jenks and Mrs. Elija Washington."

"Whoa, let me get this straight. The first time I met Detective Sattill, he was hiding behind Captain Brainerd's skirts during an interview about the Handyman Murders. Murders, which he investigated. The second time I meet the good detective, he is hiding behind the skirts of some lawyer and an assistant DA, discussing some alleged corruption—corruption that involves Detective Elija Washington and his father in law, Alphonse Mirtan. This being the same Elija Washington, whose wife, the daughter of Mr. Mirtan, was disposed of by the Handyman. Those are very connected coincidences, would not you say, Mr. Marshall? Coincidences my readers would like to know about."

"Your story must focus on the corruption. No mention can be made of the murders. To mention the murders would severely compromise another and separate police investigation. Do you understand? The corroborating commentary in your article must be listed as coming from this office. Mr. Ranck and the two detectives cannot be mentioned in your paper. Is that clear? Do we have a deal?"

With his admonition, Marshall has just sanctioned the mention of the three investigators. Newspaper people did as they please. All hell would break loose at the precinct. Wallace was so excited he had to pee. He could see the front page. He could hear the accolades of his former peers. He could taste the fruits of vindication. He was anxious to scurry away but waited for more.

Marshall pulled the attorney aside. "Mr. Ranck, what do you think? Have we told him enough to get a big splash?"

"I was thinking, you may want to drop some information about Captain Lynch's mysterious drowning in the Sound. His relationship to your on-going investigation. Just don't mention the small hole in his neck. Emphasize the drowning. I mean if we believe there is a connection between the three murders, leaking this bit would create doubt about my client as the present murderer. It would be doing him a big favor. One you could call in later. And Wallace must do all this without any reference to the three of us."

Marshall went back to Wallace. "Mr. Wallace, there is one other thing we would like you to know."

The silent mental explosion nearly removed the top of Wallace's head. His eyes expanded and contracted with each heartbeat. He had his lead to a second story, maybe even bigger than the first. Certainly, more personal. His readers would lap it up. The meeting was over. The three investigators headed for their respective homes, while Wallace rushed to the paper

"Magee, you know Wallace will include your name in his article," Franklin said. "So, stay home all day on Monday, until security for you can be arranged. Tony, you'll just have to weather the storm of intrusion and rumor. I'll be busy planning our offense for the defense. Listen, Magee do not answer the door. Stay away from the windows. If I need to reach you, I'll let the phone ring twice, hang up, and dial again. Answer the second call after eight rings, but only if the double-ring call precedes it. I know that sounds juvenile, but your safety is important. As of tomorrow morning, the bad guys will act out of panic. Panic, which could get you killed—shot or run over by a delivery truck. A low profile is a safe profile. Is that clear?"

"Sure, I guess."

"Tony, take Magee home now. Then you go directly to yours."

At the door to her unit in the Brownstone, the two past and present lovers embraced. She was safely delivered.

The intense heat of the day was beginning to wane. At home, he called Connie on her cell phone. They made a date to drive out to Brooklyn to *Tres Amis*, a Three-Star French seafood restaurant. Reservations were required. Very pricey. The stress of the weekend showed on both. Dinner was quiet. Over coffee, he took her hand and held it, like a lover who was leaving. She smiled, not knowing why. Her eyes were sad.

Home to bed.

ℰℐℰℐ

The raids and arrests began before dawn. Homes were surrounded, as the first hint of light appeared on the horizon. Doorbells were rung. Men and women in PJs and nightgowns were surprised by the men in blue with warrants for search and seizure. The dens, home offices, and garages were scoured. Boxes were carted to the trailers parked in front. The expected protestations of innocence and privacy fell on deaf ears. Pleas to call attorneys were mixed with vulgarity normally reserved for the street. The women were no less vociferous than the men. Wagons took the suspects to the Tombs.

Road Developers and three subsidiary companies were protected by a twelve-foot high cyclone fence topped by two feet of razor wire. The compound looked more like a prison than a construction company. The heavy machinery was behind the buildings. The lights and dogs were nighttime protection. No problem for the search and seizure squad—they maced the hounds, cut the fence, and secured the area. Military in precision. The locked doors were battered in. Crate upon crate of paper files, as well as three computers and a shoebox of discs, were loaded onto one of the trailers. Protesting employees were arrested if they were identifiable. Others were left to wander aimlessly like lost sheep. The decimated compound resembled a small town in Iraq.

At the bank, activity was somewhat orderly. A vice president, who arrived at seven-forty-five, was the gatekeeper. Not a suspect, she sat calmly in the break room. The vault opened automatically and promptly at eight-thirty. Papers were removed from select files and entered into a log. The offices of the bank's management were cleaned of all paperwork. The computer system relinquished file after file. All were downloaded onto police flash drives to be reviewed in the DA's office. The bank, like Road Developers, would not open for business today.

The net of the four-hour attack was staggering.

Countless rolls of crime scene tape had created festooned islands of yellow in Queens, Brooklyn, Manhattan, and Long Island. The Tombs was, for the moment, over-crowded. There would be a waiting line at the pay phone as cries for help would go out to law firms all over the city. The lawyers knew each other and each other's clients. Arraignment would be like a college reunion.

The absence of Wilson and Weaver from the roundup was critical to the event's overall success. Wiretaps and other electronic surveillance of these two would lead the DA's office to others involved in the evil doings. The good guys could get the big bad guys without having to deal away sentences. Magee's plan would work because it was based on the basest of human nature: fear and attendant overreaction.

The *Post* carried the story of the massive raids. The intricacy of the connection between the people and businesses was spelled out in great detail. The police involvement and the history of the issue were not mentioned until the second page. There were pictures from unloading the human garbage at the Tombs. Just as Wallace was told to report. However, he added uncalled for kudos—*special undercover police assistance from Detectives Anthony Sattill and Margaret Myers.* No mention of Franklin. The weasel fucked them.

"Franklin, what should I do now? What should Magee do?"

"I knew that Wallace would do more than he was told. Let me call Marshall and discuss some alternative actions. I'll call you back very soon."

The county of Brainerd was heard from. "Well, laddy, ya' got yer dick caught in it now, don't cha'? I mean, how are you going to explain yer involvement to Kelly and Echlebaum? You lied to them to make yerself seem clean. They won't take kindly to being used like that, ya' know. Hell, I don't take kindly to being used either. I went out of my way to protect you, and you were working with the DA all along. Never had the courtesy to tell yer uncle, ya little piss ant. Well, whatever happens now is yers to deal with. My hands are clean."

The old man stomped away. He had lost what little control he thought he had. Tony was taking no calls except ones from Franklin and Magee.

Franklin called. "Tony, have you spoken to Magee today."

"No. Why?"

"I can't reach her. She does not answer her phone. And, yes I've used the two-ring-hang-up-call-again-for-eight-rings procedure. Three times. I'll keep trying. Marshall and I agree that you and Magee should get out of town for a few days. Two or three days of lost time. He even volunteered to put you up in the same cottage where Hector and his family are staying. He feels it's safe and secure. But I can't reach Magee to tell her. I'm sure she's either in the shower or very sound asleep. Why don't you go to her place? I'll meet you there. I have to get directions to the castle keep from Marshall and a paper introducing us to the security guards who are there."

Tony simply got up from his desk and headed out the back door of the precinct into the parking lot. The subway was four blocks away. He ran. The local seemed to be slower than ever. He got out at the Bleeker Street stop, ran up the Brownstone's stoop, and pressed the doorbell. No answer. That was a good sign. She was not supposed to answer. He went to the pay phone on the corner and called in the prescribed manner. Still no answer. He tried the procedure three times. The dread was back. The pit of his stomach was filling with concrete.

He called Franklin's cell phone. "I'm here, but she doesn't respond to my phoning. I'm worried. My gut reaction is to break and enter. Will you cover my ass?"

"No sweat. I'll be there in twenty minutes at the latest. Get Magee."

Tony strode purposefully back to the building. He repeatedly buzzed the super. Five minutes dragged by. A young oriental couple came to the door. The supers. Tony flashed his badge and asked to be let in. The man opened the door. Tony brushed by the pair. Panic drove him. He paused at the base of the stairs.

"Get your keys to Ms. Myers's unit."

"Why do you want in there? Do you have papers?"

"The papers are on their way. I can wait. But if I wait, you'll wait in jail for about thirty days for obstruction. Get your keys, now."

The woman walked quickly to their first floor-rear apartment. She returned with a ring of keys. Tony ran up the stairs two at a time. The husband dutifully followed. At the front door to Magee's unit, the super inserted and turned to the right two keys. Tony burst in.

"Magee! Magee? *Magee*? Where are you?"

He turned the corner into the living room and there she was—nude and lashed to the wall. He rushed to her and felt the pulse in her neck. It was there. But for how much longer was in doubt. The welt on her forehead was covered with dried blood. Dried blood had clotted around her nose.

The ice pick wound was visible. There was some goo on her knee and a cigarette butt on the floor. Number three was closer to home. They were about to close the steel jaws of the trap. Was Tony next or were they simply creating enough evidence to have him convicted? And who are they?

"Call nine-one-one now. Tell them an officer is down."

He lovingly removed the tape from Magee's mouth. The tape holding her neck to the wall was peeled away. Then he removed the tape from around her neck. Finally, he cut loose the tape from the wall. He struggled to delicately raise her and hold her so she could expel the blood from her stomach and lungs. The trickle was slow. She coughed, as the sirens became audible. Suddenly there were others in the room: Kelly and Eichelberger.

"Well, I see you took care of number three."

"Help me, you guys, she's still alive."

"The paramedics are here now. They'll take care of that. Very carefully put the body down on the floor."

"Detective William Anthony Sattill Jr. you are under arrest for the murders of Ms. Charlotte Jenks and Mrs. Elija Washington, as well as the attempted murder of Detective Margaret Ann Myers. You have the right to remain silent. Anything you say can be used against you in a court of law. You have the right to an attorney. If you cannot afford an attorney, one will be appointed at no cost to you. Do you understand these rights and what I have just said?"

"I do."

Kelly harshly slapped the cuffs on Tony as Franklin enters the apartment.

"What the hell is going on here?"

"Who are you? This is a crime scene."

"I am counsel to both Detective Anthony Sattill and Detective Margaret Myers. Now answer my question."

"We have just arrested Detective Sattill for the Handyman Murders and the attempted murder of Detective Myers. By the way, your arrival is nicely timed. Seems almost planned by our perp."

"Franklin, I'm not worried, Margaret will clear me of this crime. She knows who the real attacker is."

"Officer…"

"Kelly."

"Officer Kelly, it seems to me that you arrived at the crime scene very quickly. Almost as if you were waiting for my client to arrive. How do you explain that?"

"My partner and I followed Detective Sattill. We've been following him for a while now. We knew he would lead us to his next crime. And we were right."

The paramedics were poring over Magee's inert form. They wrapped her in blankets and flash a penlight in her eyes. The eyes were dilated and non-responsive to light. But she was not dead—yet.

"ER stat! She is very weak. Vitals are barely registering."

"Detective Sattill, you're off to the Tombs. Arraignment will be tomorrow. You can spend a pleasant night with some of the lowlife you helped bust this morning. It should be a fun-filled time."

"Tony, I'll be waiting for your arrival at the Tombs. Be calm. Oh, and officers—I'll be watching."

Franklin headed for the DA's office. He needed a favor from Marshall. Tony needed a big favor. Tony needed to be placed where he could be safe until tomorrow. Some cell with rapists and murders. Not the cell with the suspects from the Road Developers and First Bank arrests. Marshall understood, but he was loath to piss off the police any more than he had today. He also realized that Tony's arrest would compromise the big case, which was now oh-so-public. He needed the corruption case to make his case for the future. The debate he faced was whether to protect Tony and keep information out of the corruption case or to include Tony and have the case be rent asunder by an aggressive defense attorney, like Franklin.

Marshall's decision to include Tony and risk the case was based, in part, on Franklin's assurances that the police had nothing of substantive value. In fact, Franklin argued that the cops had tainted evidence pushed forward by the same SIU that had guided Wilson and Weaver. Marshall decided to stand in front of Tony.

The press had a field day. *Good cop goes bad.* The *News* scoops the *Post* and poked fun at Wallace's story.

Better to wait a day and be right than to rush to judgment and miss the guilty.

At the arraignment, $1,000,000 bail was requested based upon the heinous nature of the multiple murders. The assistant DA assigned to the case was playing hard-ball. Franklin argued that his client was cooperating with the district attorney's office in an unrelated matter, he would not leave the jurisdiction, and he had been, until this fabricated allegation, an exemplary police officer. Bail was set at $750,000. Another amount out of Tony's reach.

As he was led away by the bailiff, the Brens approached Franklin and whispered to him. He turned to Tony and smiled. A certified check for $75,000 would be hand delivered to the clerk at the jail in one hour. Amway had been very, very good to them. And now Tony. Tony would be free but on a very short tether. He and Franklin would be joined at the hip. They decided not to go up-state. That would help Marshall's appearance of detach-ment. Also, while they plotted their defense, they didn't want to be surrounded by the enemy's ears. Connie awaited her lover's release. She, Franklin, and Tony headed off to The Bluffs. Slightly illegal to leave the state of New York, but arguably reasonable, because the ac-cused's lawyer would be with the accused at all times. Computers, all of the files, and two cell phones. The de-fense had a lot to prepare. The drive was quiet. The skies portended the time at the shore.

"Tony, we need to sit in a quiet place and review all the material we have. So, Ms. Wilhaus, if you'll forgive us, we need to claim the sunroom as our conference room."

Tony headed upstairs to retrieve his stash of computer, papers, and the tape from the closet. The lockbox was beneath his suitcase. He had a vague feeling something was out of place. Not pit of the stomach dread, but a mental perception. Downstairs, the war room was readied. Laptops were fired up. The micro-recorder was plugged in. Papers were placed in stacks.

"As I see it, the case against you hinges on some arcane physical evidence and your whereabouts during the events. There is clearly no motive, and the police have yet to find a weapon. Any link with the death of Captain Lynch will weaken their case against you. So, we must be ready to make a very strong link between the murders of Lynch and the two women to create doubt and, therefore, destroy their case against you. We can prove that you did not know him and that, during the time he was tanked, you were nowhere around. Exactly where were you on Memorial Day weekend five years ago?"

"I was…with Detective Myers. We had gone away for a long weekend. Putney, Vermont, I believe. I charged everything on my AmEx. We can get the signed receipts."

"Well, hopefully, she will be able to verify everything when we get back to the city. I will reach out at every four hours to ascertain her status. When she recovers, we must head back to the city immediately. We have to get to her before Kelly and Echlebaum do. Or else they can twist whatever she says to suit their needs, regardless of your innocence. Tony, do you think these two, Mutt and Jeff as you call them, were sent into the fray to protect Wilson and Weaver? Hear me out. Someone, say Captain Brainerd, starts you on an investigation of Washington. Let's say Brainerd does this to help your career and to solidify his. He has no proof of any real wrongdoing, but he knows that everybody is dirty. Rierdan retires. That leaves you and Washington available for the top spot in Manhattan CAT. If Washington's dirty laundry is hung on the line, you remain clean. You are promoted. You are beholden to Brainerd. Stranger things have been done to secure allies.

"Now, SIU gets wind of your investigation into Washington. But they don't know about his post-facto entry into the case file because they never looked. Arrogance. They fear that you'll turn up something against Wilson and Weaver, something given up by Washington. So, to protect their own, they attack you from two sides. They make it easy for you to damn Washington and imply the damnation of Wilson and Weaver. But, they control just what information you can access. So, they think. Simultaneously, they attack you as the murderer. Investigate the investigator, plant evidence, and generally rig the case against you. Their plan is to have you fall as the murderer. Your case against Washington would stop with him, so he falls. Wilson and Weaver are protected as victims of the ranting and flailing of two fallen cops."

"That's way out, counselor. The workings of the inner circle of power are beyond my ken. So, it could be possible. But what went wrong?"

"What went wrong is that Washington planted the damaging information in the file and you discovered it. What went wrong is that you taped Washington's confessional Q and A. What went wrong is that we went to Assistant DA Marshall before SIU could collapse the wall on you. Now they're scrambling. Scramblers are the most dangerous adversaries because they are big risk takers. They will do anything to win. These guys will plant evidence. They will intimidate a witness. They will murder the weakest link in their organization."

"Do you think they would kill a witness? Do you think they would kill Magee?"

"Not with patrolmen from the two-seven in her room twenty-four/seven. Before we left, Marshall and I agreed that her own would best protect her. He called Captain Elliot. Her safety is assured. I have Elliot's cell number. He expects a call every four hours. He will then radio the two men on guard and call me with their status report. If something befalls Magee, the men on duty will notify Elliot, and he will call me. We can do nothing on this front but wait."

"We must do something."

"We must prepare for your interview at the DA's office on Monday. As I understand it, the assistant assigned to the case is excruciatingly zealous and similarly ambitious. Virginia Nunno will come at you with both barrels. Evidence, the requested bail of one million. To make the case, she'll have to kill your alibis and place you at the scenes. We'll get to Connie in a minute. I realize that I'll have to isolate her response. I'm sure she doesn't need to know that you were having dinner with Magee prior to Mrs. Washington's murder. My feeling is that Kelly and Echlebaum got some part of your body or bodily fluids from somewhere other than the crime scenes. Where could they have gotten hair?"

"My desk."

"What?"

"Occasionally, hair from my head and beard will fall on my desk. Also, I have this habit of plucking eyebrow hair when I am nervous. Anybody could come by my desk and lift numerous hairs. Come to think of it, when Brainerd and I were interviewing Wallace, those two were in the observation room. They could have gone over to my desk and scoured it for hair."

"They then could have three different hairs to plant and find. Run DNAs on all three. Viola! A match. The same guy was at every murder scene. Now they go to your desk again, find some more hair. Bingo! You are that same guy. Now how about fingerprints?"

"My personnel records and my gun permit have my prints. My missing coffee mug has my prints. Everything in, on, and around my desk has my prints. But how do they get the prints to the crime scenes? Besides, my team was all over the area."

"They take special cellophane tape. Rub off your prints from your mug, telephone, and desk. Then take the tape to the crime scenes after your team was there and press it on to a strong, non-porous surface like a sink, metal handle, or tile wall. A partial of the print comes off on the hard surface. With multiple partials at each scene, enough is extracted to place you at the murders. Now they have two independent corroborating forms of evidence."

"How do you know all this?"

"The hair bit is not too difficult to figure out. No offense, but you just did. The fingerprint trick is part of an advanced criminality course I took years ago. A lecturer from Holland enthralled us with tricks seen in Europe but unknown to US law enforcement, I think. Hell, I even used it once during some dirty tricks that were part of a corporate take-over we nipped in the bud. The problems with the tape trick are two-fold: the cellophane can substantially distort the print in application and reapplication process, and the cellophane can leave adhesive residue around and on the print. The residue is noticeable on the surface with a good scope. So, if they did this and didn't destroy the surface we got 'em."

"How can we prove they planted the hair?"

"I don't know the answer to that—yet. Let me think on that subject for a while. We may not need to prove they planted your hair. Just create the impression that they could have done it, due to their motivation to frame you. All of this assumes that they cannot prove you had a motive. You didn't have a motive, did you?"

"I have no motive."

"They can always create one or two. So, we'll have to be prepared to rebut their assertions."

"No motives. No weapon. Good alibis. Or, at least, alibi. And only hair at the scenes. Their case is not iron-clad. I know Assistant DA Nunno is a hothead and has an ego and desire bigger than Marshall's. We could be in for an ugly and protracted fight."

"There are two other items, which I don't understand. The semen and the cigarette butts. You don't smoke. So, I think the butts are red herrings planted by the real killer or killers. Since there were three different brands, the red herring theory will hold. We will need to re-canvass the neighbors and the supers to double-check the comings and goings associated with the three timeframes. That's easy. I'll call a PI I know, who works good and fast. Now the semen. My theory is that since the cigarette butts are red herrings, the semen deposits are also. The cops secure hair samples from you. They plant the hair samples at the scenes. DNA tests are run on both sets of hair samples. The cops get the match they knew they would. Then they bogey the lab report to reflect that the tests in the lab were run on semen and hair, not hair alone. The importance is the difference between lab test results and lab reports. Whammo, they have what appears to be very solid proof of your evil deeds. But if we can create doubt about the fingerprints, cigarette butts, we can create doubt about the hair. If we can create doubt about the hair and the lab tests, we can create doubt about the semen. All of this will be aided by our ability to outline a conspiracy. The NYPD SIU protecting its own conspires to crush a fearless investigator. We have our work cut out for us."

"I obviously trust you with my life. I'll do whatever it takes to get you the information you need. If it requires man-hours, I have a lot of markers out in the force. There are a lot of people who would be willing to help me. We can even go to the medical examiner's office. Dr. Cut Up, sorry Dr. Minnig, is a square shooter. She would never compromise her reputation. I can call her to get the complete lab reports."

"Okay, and while you're doing that—from your room—I'll talk to Connie."

Connie and Tony trade places in the house.

"We'll need to you call as an alibi witness, Connie. So, would you tell me, were you with Tony on the night prior to the discovery of the murdered Charlotte Jenks? That would be the evening of June first?"

"Yes, I was with Tony."

"What did you and Tony do that evening?"

"We met after work, had dinner at PJ Melons, and went home to bed."

"What time did you have dinner?"

"We met at the restaurant at nine-thirty. I had to work late. I assume Tony did also."

Franklin realizes there is a time gap, which Tony will have to explain. Franklin will have to get corroborating testimony about Tony's presence at the precinct until at least nine from his colleagues.

"Thank you."

"Aren't you going to ask me about the evening of July sixteenth? Because I have no idea where Tony was that night until he got home. And, it was late when he did."

"No, that won't be necessary."

Why is she forthcoming with non-information? What is she really saying? It will be a risk using Connie as ali-

bi support for Tony. She could blow the entire alibi defense. Is she angry with Tony? Does she know about Magee? She will need to be well-coached before she goes on the stand. Stick to what she knows.

CHAPTER 12

12 Center Street:

Franklin called Captain Elliot. Still, nothing to report. The patient was in critical condition. She had been stabilized. Neither upgraded nor downgraded since her arrival at St. Luke's. The doctors had told Elliot that the detective lost a great deal of blood. The blood loss caused a loss of oxygen to the brain. Plus, the patient suffered a substantial blunt trauma to the frontal lobe. The brain had been damaged. How much damage the brain suffered, the doctors would not even speculate. There had been an infusion of new, acceptable blood, but there had not been a noticeable and positive impact on brain functions. Life support was absolutely necessary. She was being monitored very closely for any sign of improvement.

Elliot guessed that if there was no improvement in the detective's condition within the next seventy-two hours, the doctors might want to operate. Or, they might want to designate her as brain dead. Then the issue became one of plug pulling. This would be a decision for her parents. The prospects were not good.

The one eyewitness might die before she could exonerate the accused perpetrator and point the finger at the real one. She would also be unable to supply an alibi for Tony's whereabouts on the evening prior to Chakika Washington's murder, as well as the murder of Patrick Lynch. Franklin decided not to tell Tony.

"How is Magee? Can we see her when we're in town on Monday?"

"Captain Elliot reports that she is resting comfortably and that the attending physicians are guardedly optimistic."

"When will she be able to tell Kelly and Echlebaum the truth about her attacker?"

"The doctors hope Magee will be able to be interviewed later in the week. Whenever it is, we want to be there before Mutt and Jeff."

Connie went home with the Brens on Sunday evening. Franklin and Tony ate dinner in silence. The Monday morning ride to the city was very quiet. The two were ushered into Assistant DA Nunno's office. Her attire and seated attitude told Franklin all he needed to know about her approach to negotiation: she would state her position and then dig in her heels. There would be no flexibility, at least during the first session. The key to dealing with this sort of combatant was to give up hints of information that could be pursued before the second sit down. If this process could be repeated, Franklin could get almost all of what he wants. Couldn't give her too much information at one time, or be too direct. Certainly, couldn't give her all of what Franklin knew over the course of the ordeal. Rather, he had to let her discover his points as if they were her own. Very delicate.

"Good morning Mr. Ranck, Detective Sattill. Let's get right to the heart of the matter. Let me give you an assessment as to the strength of our case. We have irrefutable physical evidence that links Detective Sattill to each of the crime scenes. We know there are large holes in the alibis dealing with his whereabouts prior to the murders. So we have opportunity. And we are close to finding the weapon of choice."

"With all of this hard evidence against my client, there appears to be no reason for a trial, except…"

"Except, what Mr. Ranck?"

"Except number one: there are a number of alternate theories, which can be introduced to create enough doubt in the minds of two or three jurors. My client is a victim of a very profound and far-reaching police conspiracy. Captains and commanders are about to get their asses kicked by the investigation into Road Developers and First Bank of Long Island. These same captains and commanders set about to frame my client, so as to taint his testimony in Assistant DA Marshall's investigation. I can prove this. Doubt in the jurors' minds will destroy your case. Except number two: your physical evidence is tainted at best. Except number three: the district attorney reached out to my client for his help in unraveling a case his good office has been sputtering on for about two years. Your boss owes my client. Except, except, except."

"Nice try counselor, but no cigar."

"Then, let us go to trial. Set the date at your convenience. We're ready now. Until that time, thanks for your time."

Tony and Franklin got up to leave.

"Please, be back in this office on Wednesday at nine a.m.," Virginia Nunno cordially barked. "We'll discuss this matter further. Good day."

"What just happened?"

"Our position was probed. Assistant DA Nunno laid down a burst of gunfire at our feet to see us jump. We didn't. We gave her hints of our knowledge—so she thinks. Now she'll go back to her sources and dig deeper so that she will in a stronger position to attack and defeat us. What she doesn't know is that when she digs into these areas, she will see how weak her case really is. I can put pressure on her from above if need be. But, not yet. That trump card will have to wait until after our second meeting. Until then, we'll just go about the business of an offensive defense. Now go home and rest. I'll call you if I hear anything about Magee."

Tony decided to clean the apartment and do some laundry. Anxiety bred ennui. Ennui bred boredom. Boredom bred nesting. Dusting, vacuuming, and scouring surfaces were nearly Puritanical. The work was solitary. It was necessary for the maintenance of his life, or at least his environment. He could see the results of his work, so he could bask in the glow of accomplishment. Plus, his mate would praise him for his industriousness. The non-Puritanical side of the endeavor was that, instead of praying or contemplating his shortcomings, he could think about his life's predicament and how to extricate himself from it. He had no answers. Laundry was begun as an aside to the cleaning. Yes, he could do two things at once. Whites. Darks. Coloreds. Delicates. Four loads of wash and four loads of drying took up the afternoon. He was exhausted when Connie called.

"You're doing *what*?"

"When you get home, I'll even have a great meal ready for the table."

"Well, I'm sorry to report that I won't be home until well after ten. We're in the final stages. Two weeks and we're on the street and in the media. Then the tours for interested investors. Presentations every day. The *circus glutimus maximus*. If we are properly rehearsed and, therefore, successful, we will have the go for our IPO within a few months. Papers are going to authorities and regulators the day after tomorrow. So, *Mister Mom*, I can only say, I'll see ya' when I see ya'."

"Okay, honey, good luck. We can do dinner on Wednesday."

"It's a date."

Puritanical piety to purposeless self-pity in thirty seconds. He continued to redistribute the clean clothes. She liked T-shirts on hangers. His were rolled. His socks were rolled. Hers were folded. The closet seemed smaller and more crowded than he remembered. Probably because he never really noticed the space. As Tony turned to fetch more socks and tees, his foot smacked one of Connie's many sports bags. He stumbled but didn't fall. The hand weights, five pounders, inside her bag were not kind to his foot. He stubbed his toe and cursed the pain. The bag was shoved underneath some skirts and next to Connie's bureau. Connie's work-out stuff was like his computer. He pillaged the fridge, conquering a chicken breast and salad from last Thursday. He was really bored and began to think of Magee. What harm would there be in a visit? A lot of harm. He could see the headline tomorrow—*Attacker Stalks Victim.*

Wallace, Kelly, and Echlebaum would have a field day. They would make his visit an admission of guilt. Tony had lost complete control of his life. The portent of doom from surrounding forces was real. The shadows were fading, and the demons were emerging. He had to sit and take whatever they dish out.

The next day had twenty-four hours in it before noon. Tony called Franklin. No improvement in Magee's condition. She was just there. Franklin indicated that her parents were sitting vigil and that they would have to make some tough decisions in the next few days. The jolt to Tony's gut was powerful. If Magee died, his past and present lover died. If Magee died, his defense died. There would be no corroborating testimony. No alibi. Also, the DA would be less inclined to be cooperative for just Tony, whereas the team of Tony and Magee could have extracted sympathy from the public and therefore put pressure on the DA. Depression took over from panic. The urge to dive into the bottle or go white lining was strong. He had to be with Franklin to be safe from himself. Franklin understood. The two would be roommates for a while. Connie understood. The next morning took a week to arrive. The subway trip to 12 Center Street took a day. The elevator ride and walk down the hall consumed two hours. Life in slo-mo land was no fun.

"Well, what do have to offer us today, Ms. Nunno?"

"A hard dose of reality, Mr. Ranck. We have confirmed our extensive evidence that your client was at the two murder scenes. We have fingerprints and we have DNA from the semen he left on the victims. In the search of Detective Sattill's apartment, the police discovered a vial of GHB, the same drug used to incapacitate the two victims. And, they found an ornate silver ice pick, which had been recently scrubbed clean. We are checking it for blood residue. We have him cold."

"What you have is evidence planted by the same police who have been ordered to find him guilty, regardless of the truth. What else did Kelly and Echlebaum find? A hit list? There is no motive for my client to kill these two women. But there is a strong motive to discredit him. Did you ask Assistant DA Marshall about the activities of the police thugs, Wilson and Weaver, after the raid on the bank and the builder? I'll bet they are scurrying around like rats in a barn on fire. And I'll bet they have put extra pressure on their friends, Kelly and Echlebaum. So, these two went out and bought some GHB and an ice pick. Put some blood, which matches Detective Myers's blood type, on the pick and wash it, then have the supposed weapon analyzed for victims' blood. With rigged DNA tests, they have what appears to be ironclad evidence. God, Ms. Nunno. It's all too easy. You are being led around by two stooges who report to the NYPD SIU, who, in turn, desperately want my client found guilty and off their collective ass. Whatever evidence you think you may have does not fit the attack on Detective Myers. Why was she hit on the head? Because she fought. The other two didn't. Why would a friend fight a friend? Would not a lover submit to a lover? What about retired Captain Lynch? The same MO. Did Sattill kill someone he didn't even know? Did my client kill Captain Lynch from four hundred miles away? Why? Is there GHB in Detective Myers's system? If so, why the bump on the head? Is Detective Myers a victim of a copycat? Is she the victim of Kelly and Echlebaum? That would explain their incredibly rapid arrival and that of the paramedics. The cops alerted them before my client got to the scene. The cops were waiting for my client because they knew my client would come to the woman they had attacked.

"The power elite is protecting its collective ass by getting you to attack Detective Sattill. What I have just said will create doubt in the minds of a few jurors. Hell, all I need is one. But my defense is so strong, I'll bet you that when you poll the jurors, you'll find out that at least five are for immediate acquittal. Look, we want what you want. We want the truth. Justice will follow. To get to the truth, I suggest we have a sit down with Assistant DA Marshall and see how much the cases dovetail. See if your boss, DA Price, can understand the viability of the conspiracy. Once he sees that I am right, we will cooperate in your investigation, just as we did in the corruption investigation."

"I will talk to both the gentlemen. But I can't promise anything. Let's say we get back together tomorrow at this time. Pending the meeting, we can go forward to trial."

"See you tomorrow."

Franklin's pace was rapid as they exited the building. He stopped Tony on the steps. "We have punched a hole in her titanium breastplate. She can smell kudos based on her cracking a conspiracy case. Price will see his future in this three-headed hydra—white collar crime, the mob, and dirty cops. The stuff of a DA's dreams. He can combine the two cases, prosecute the new, bigger case himself, and award Marshall and Nunno the privilege of sharing the second chair. They all win. We go away. Very tidy.

"We must talk to Dr. Minnig about the DNA tests before the DA's office gets to her," Tony responded.

The building that housed the morgue and the medical examiner's workshop had three stories above ground and three below. The public saw the beautiful structure above ground, while the distasteful work was done in the sterile catacombs underground. Being underground cut down on the electricity needed to run the AC. Exhaust fans and air purifiers were cheaper than AC. Dr. Cut Up was waiting in her office.

She was all business, but more personable than the

DA. The good doctor looked nothing like her voice would indicate. She looked like a pixy. Small. Pale skin. Blonde hair. Bangs and a ponytail. Delicate blue eyes. High cheekbones and a friendly smile. She was attractive in a teenage Grace Kelly look-alike way. Certainly not the look of a sultry siren. "Mr. Ranck. I have checked and double-checked the lab reports on the DNA and can find no errors. The DNA from the items from the scenes matches the DNA from the items found at the detective's desk."

"Of course the DNAs match, Doctor. The cops took the multiple samples of the hair and submitted it as if it had been found at both places when, in reality, it was found only at the detective's desk. Kelly and Echlebaum planted evidence. They planted fingerprints. They are working very hard to frame him."

"That explains the hair, sir. But it does not explain the semen. The semen's DNA, too, is a match for the hair's DNA."

"I'll give you an explanation for the apparent match. You submitted the semen for DNA matching. Am I correct?"

"Yes, we did that. Then the police secured the remainder of our samples. They took the remainder immediately after we received it from the crime scenes. I believe they submitted it for testing by an outside lab."

"We know it was semen from the crime scenes. But what if the two lieutenants persuaded the outside lab to issue a report that was accurate on findings, just inaccurate on the material? Why did they respond to the crimes so quickly? How did they know to acquire the semen from both scenes and ask a lab to compare the samples— perhaps before they were officially on the cases? What is the name of the lab that supplied the test results?"

"NeoBio Analysis. It's located in Queens. We've used them before. Their work meets our standards. Here's the address. A contact would be Dr. Walter Wilson. Now, let me get this straight. We test the DNA. We find no match. NeoBio Analysis tests the DNA, and they find a match to hairs. Both the hair and the semen are from the crime scenes. Where did they get the hair to create a match with the killer?"

"I think we know. We just have to make sure all roads do not lead to the Roman."

The doctor's name struck fear in Franklin's heart. Wilson. It was all too convenient. The door and windows of NeoBio Analysis were covered with metal gates. Both the gate and the front door were locked. After ten minutes, no one responded to the buzzer. Tony and Franklin headed home, concerned. Franklin decided to call his PI and ask him to sit on NeoBio Analysis first thing tomorrow morning.

"Franklin, I understand why you claimed you left the high-flying corporate legal world—burn out. But my police instincts tell me there was more. Now that I've shown you mine, will you show me yours?"

"What happened there and then should be of no concern to you. What should be of concern is only what will happen in the next few days, weeks, and months. I will tell you this. I saw more dishonesty, corruption, and hidden agendas while serving my ever-so-proper corporate clients than I have since I left Ali Baba's house. So, without being rude, let's focus on you."

"I guess what heightens my curiosity is how you are handling my case. You seem to be two steps ahead of them and me. You also seem to enjoy this endeavor more than would be expected. Why?"

"Being ahead of others has always been my strength. I have the ability to simultaneously view events, facts, and arguments from numerous points-of-view. I can imagine causes of events which others wouldn't consider. For every event, there are normally several viable causes. I can sense from whence people are coming in their arguments. I can think like they are thinking. I can mentally want what they want. I can race six steps ahead to determine where they want to be. If this scenario fits my objective, I do nothing. If I want them to wind up in a different place, I lead them. I can do all of this because I am totally immersed in the case or situation. From their point-of-view and mine. I never stop thinking about it from all points-of-view—yours, mine, the DA's, the cops, you name it. I never stop imagining. Never stop leading—you and them. I want to win, and I want you to win. And, just as much, I want them to lose. I want the bad guys, the cops, the killer, and corrupt officials to lose. I want to crush them. Shit, that sounds like my mantra of the sixties. Yes, I'm arrogant. It's because I'm good. That's why I'm here with you. You need me."

The volume of Franklin's voice had gone from conversational to protest leader. But the bullhorn and soapbox were missing. Tony headed home for the evening. Dinner alone again. Aloneness bred depression. He needed to talk to someone. Be with someone. He wanted to visit Magee. Ask her forgiveness for getting her involved. For her being hurt. If she forgave him, he could sleep. Tonight sleep would be induced by a half bottle of Oban.

He arrived at 12 Center Street thirty minutes early. He wanted the process to speed up. Franklin was ten minutes late. He liked the upper hand of making his opponent wait. Time control.

"Mr. Ranck, good morning. Good morning, Detective. I think we can see some light at the end of the tunnel."

Franklin's expression did not change, although the victory flag was visible. Tony was puzzled.

"What I'm saying is that, upon a painstaking analysis of all the facts of the case—as well as new information, which has come to our attention—we feel it is in the best interest of the people of New York to try to settle this matter without a protracted and expensive court battle." Assistant DA Nunno held her head high even in defeat.

"What are you offering my client?"

"That will be up to District Attorney Price. I am empowered to prepare a recommendation for his review."

Franklin was not done with the battle yet. "Fair enough. Since you've got *bupkus* against my client, I'm sure you will recommend dropping the case altogether. Plus, you can claim the plum of nailing Kelly and Echlebaum. I don't care what charges you bring against them."

"Well, we'll see about that."

"Okay, let us start with your so-called irrefutable evidence. Motive and alibis."

Every aspect of the case was discussed in detail. The DA's position was on the table. Franklin countered it. Then Franklin's counter was countered. This back and forth, give and take went on for three hours. The only interruptions were for coffee and to pee. The buzzer interrupted Ms. Nunno mid-sentence.

"Yes, thank you. Another wrinkle. Detective Myers's parents may decide to take her off life support and let her die. There is nothing we can do. The problem now is that this event raises a bigger issue. Kelly and Echlebaum will ratchet up their attack on Detective Sattill since they were at the crime scene. Undoubtedly, they'll go public with a cry for a speedy trial. All of this will happen too quickly. It will be a damage control nightmare. But the firestorm will be over just as quickly when we go public."

"May I make a phone call to my PI?"

"Sure. Why?"

"Some additional light to be shed on the case against the SIU."

"Let's all take a ten-minute break."

The dead were rising to the status of magnanimous queen. When Franklin returned, he was almost aglow. "Dr. Walter Wilson is the brother of a certain Lieutenant Wilson, who works at One Police Plaza. The boys were adopted by Eugene Eichelberger, the deceased former president of First Bank of Long Island. The trail of the DNA proof is clear. The semen is a red herring. Hair is the only body part of Detective Sattill to be subjected to DNA analyses. The analysis from NeoBio Analysis is accurate, but the report false. Dr. Wilson's testimony will confirm there was no semen, only hair."

Nunno nodded. "We will visit Doctor Wilson after we are done here. Assistant District Attorney Marshall has shared with us that, immediately after the raids conducted last week, Lieutenants Wilson and Weaver were sequestered at One Police Plaza from seven a.m. to noon. They obviously went there for counsel. To be told what to do. And they did what they were told. Upon leaving, they went to their respective homes where they have stayed since. To the best of our knowledge, they have had no contact with the world outside their homes. We are watching their houses and have monitored their phones and computer lines. They have gone silent. Now, this is what I'm going to do. We will summarize our findings and beliefs as of this morning in the form of a recommendation to my boss. If you would like to come back tomorrow at nine a.m., you can review the document and confirm your agreement."

Tony couldn't think of Magee dying. The depression would divert him from his primary goal; saving his ass. His body began to relax. The muscles in his shoulders softened. His hearing intensified and his vision became sharper. He could come out of himself. The subway ride back to his place was fast and friendly. His pace quickened. Next week, he'd be able to return to duty. This weekend, he could revel in the surf and sun. He wanted to go to The Bluffs tonight.

Connie agreed that an extra day of R and R was just the tonic. She got home about six. They left the apartment at six-thirty. Two bags—his small gym bag and her leather bag were tossed in the back seat. She brought no work. This would be a tonic for her, too. The uneventful drive was followed by a dinner of fresh bluefish, angel-hair pasta, Jersey tomatoes, and many drinks. The celebration was long overdue. Nothing was said of the recent ordeal. Nothing needed to be said. Nightcaps on the deck. Tony fell asleep under the stars.

His pager was vibrating madly. It was one a.m. Who the hell would page him at this hour? Franklin.

Tony called. "What can't wait until later today?"

"The DA got to Dr. Wilson. He steadfastly maintains that NeoBio Analysis did run a DNA analysis on both semen and hair. The samples of each are not readily available. DA Nunno is unable to break his story. She informed me that the deal is off the table for now. There are just too many logic-gaps in our theory. She needs time to pull together more evidence. I tried to convince her that it was very convenient that the samples are not available. Just like it is very convenient that the doctor is the brother of one of our suspects. She is buying none of it. She won't take another step until we clarify this confusion, as she calls it. You're still the suspect, Tony. I need time to unravel this conundrum. I'm coming down to be with you tomorrow. I'll be on the train that gets into Bayhead Station at one-fifteen. Can you pick me up? In the meantime, relax."

Tony had just had hot bamboo shoots inserted beneath his fingernails and was told to relax at the same moment. Those were two things he couldn't do at once. Sleep was out of the question. So was booze. Thinking could only be done with a clear head. He headed to the shoreline for a walk. The beach near the water was firm, so leg fatigue was not a factor. Mental fatigue was. Emotional fatigue was the bigger factor. When he reached the lighthouse at the end of the island, he turned and headed for home.

How can we break Dr. Wilson's lie? What pressure can be applied to let the truth flow? License renewal? Code violations? What promise can be made to make it worth Dr. Wilson's while to cooperate? Contracts with the city? Big money? What would Magee say? How would she handle this twist? How would she think about the problem?

She'd first want to be absolutely sure it was not Tony's semen. Okay. There was semen at the two scenes.

Questions: Was it left by the murderer? Or was it planted between the time the victim was murdered and the time the CAT squad was called? If the latter, by whom? Fact: something was analyzed by NeoBio Analysis. Questions: Was it hair alone? Was it hair and semen? What if the lab analyzed hair and semen and the semen came from the crime scenes? But what if the results of the DNA analyses, that is to say, the reports, were incorrectly labeled. Lieutenant Wilson calls his brother. The cop brother, who had their stepfather killed in prison, tells the doctor brother to analyze both hair and semen. Both supposedly from the crime scenes. Let every-

body in the lab see the semen and the process of its analysis. Even make a show of it. The doctor, himself, runs the analyses. He then takes his findings and creates a third report. This third report, the one turned over to his brother, is based on the facts of the hair analysis alone. But it is issued as if were the hair and semen analyses. This is simple sleight of hand—laboratory legerdemain. Doctor Wilson then destroys all evidence of the two analyses. The winner is NYPD SIU. And the loser is the man with the fallen hair—Detective Sattill. The key to cracking the mystery is to find the assistant who ran the two discarded analyses.

Tony's pace quickened to a jog. A death-inducing millstone had been lifted from his neck. He stopped and stared at the first light. Prayer was not feasible for him. So he thanked Magee.

CHAPTER 13

43 Ocean Drive:

I didn't realize the trains to this part of the world eschewed AC."

Franklin's entire body looked wrinkled, not just his clothes. He was beginning to show the effects of negotiating the case. He tossed his bag on the back seat. The car's AC was cranked. Franklin began to shiver. "I must sound menopausal, but now I'm cold. Could you turn down the air conditioning? I'm sure my body will be in synch with the temperature of its environment when we get to the house."

Tony took Franklin's stuff to the room formerly shared by Charlotte and Bill and then met his lawyer in the sunroom.

Connie was upstairs asleep or reading her texts.

Tony spelled out his theory of the duped DNA tests.

Franklin was impressed. "Very good for a cop. Let me call my PI and have him go out to NeoBio Analysis right now. Then we can discuss another approach."

Call made, he held while the PI determined a name to see. Doctor Wilson was not in today. Tonya Miller performed the semen DNA analysis. The PI would report to Franklin this evening.

"What is this other approach?"

"First I have to tell you that Magee expired last evening at seven-thirty p.m. An autopsy will be performed on her body, which will then be sent to a funeral home near her parents. I believe they have plans to cremate Magee's remains and place them in a church crypt somewhere on Long Island. When this is all over, and you are exonerated, I'm sure they would like to see you."

The reality struck Tony hard. Was this the demon or just of the demons, which were waiting to devour him. Tears trickled down both cheeks. Why the hell did he ever get her involved in this mess? If he had kept her out of it, she would be alive. Given who she was, and who she was for Tony, she should have never been uninvolved. But she wanted to be involved because of who she was to Tony.

"If you want to take a break, we can. Okay, what I'm about to say will infuriate you. So hear me out before you explode. Let us assume that the lab analyzed the semen, which your CAT squad found at the crime scenes. And let us assume that the semen is yours. Now we must learn how it got from you to the knees of the victims."

"What in God's name are you saying? You know I'm innocent. You know it's not my semen. Are you 'One Toke Over the Line'? Are you crazy?"

"I told you this would infuriate you. We have to explore all avenues. Please understand that my job and my passion are to protect you from jail. To protect you from the needle and gurney. To do this, I must look at the facts from every conceivable angle, no matter how crazy it may appear to others. I have to uncover the truth to get you justice."

"Rant on, Macbeth."

"If the semen is yours, how did it get there? Either you put it there, or someone else did. Assuming for the moment that you did not because you told me you do not store the stuff—"

"Thanks a bunch."

"—assuming for the moment that you did not leave the calling card, it was left by someone else. Someone who has access to your precious bodily fluids. The person who comes to mind first is Connie."

"Impossible. What reason would she have to kill the three women and to harm me in the process? I mean, my God, we're going to be married next year. You're crazy."

"I don't know her reasons—yet. The critical questions are: What do we know about Connie? Who was she before she met you? Who is her circle of friends beyond you? Who is her family? What would be her motivation?"

"Yeah, what?"

"A few days ago, I began looking into Connie's life

and her past. Not much threatening or foreboding about her present—The Seven Sisters, you, and that's about it. But here's the interesting part. She has no past. All stored information about her goes no farther back than five years. This is about the time you two met. We can't even find her college record. If she had been a cheerleader at Penn State, it was under an assumed name and a different face. Both of which are possible. Social Security shows her contributions beginning five years ago. Her driver's license was applied for five years ago. She signed her first apartment lease five years ago. It's as if she were born a mature woman five years ago. This is disconcerting."

"How is that possible? She's told me about her college life. Previous jobs, a few old boyfriends. Her parents lived in Ephrata, a small town outside of Lancaster, Pennsylvania. They're dead now. Some sort of an auto accident. She showed me pictures of her folks, her brother, and herself as a small child."

"I don't know what you saw, but it has no basis in my understanding of reality. The reality is that Connie has been reinvented by someone or some organization. So, I checked her name. Constance Angelica Wilhaus. No birth records in New York, Pennsylvania, or any of the other forty-eight states for a female live birth with that name and her age. I contacted an old friend with the FBI and asked her if she knew of anyone who fit Connie's description who was in the witness protection program. She ran the records that she could access and found no one. Now there are a few records that she could not access, but her gut is that your girlfriend is a figment of someone else's imagination. The net of all my digging is that we don't really know who or what Connie is."

"I won't believe this bull. I can't believe it. I can't believe you did this digging behind my back. I can't believe that you found nothing about Connie's past. I can't believe that she would do what you are claiming she did."

"When you and Connie make love, do you use protection?"

"Yes, I wear a condom."

"The perfect vehicle to collect and save your semen for deposit later."

"Semen dries quickly when exposed to air."

"It can be saved in a lid-tight vial in a freezer for a few days."

"This is crazy. You can paint this picture of an alien who collects semen from her Earthly lover so it can be left as evidence at murders, which she commits for no apparent reason. DA Nunno would pee herself while laughing at this theory of yours—if you ever presented it."

"If we can find out who Connie really is, we'll have the answers to all of our questions. I have several people digging deeper into her past. They will phone me when they have anything to report. So, while others are exploring the workings at the lab and the identity of your lady friend, we should be preparing for our meeting with DA Nunno on Monday. Let's go for a walk so we won't be heard or interrupted."

They retraced Tony's steps of twelve hours ago and

returned to the bedroom to stand at Connie's blanket three hours after their start. Many questions posed. Not as many answers given.

"Hey, sweetie. Do you know if the Brens are coming down this weekend?"

"I've not heard from them since last weekend after they bailed you out."

Franklin cleared his throat. "Listen, you two, let's have dinner out tonight before the hurly-burly crowd rushes in. My treat. Tony and I have some more work tomorrow. Not much, about a half a day. Then he's yours, Connie. I'll just disappear into some singles bar and see if I can work my magic. Hope you guys don't mind."

Connie laughed. "Franklin, you closet swinger, of course, we don't mind. Don't be ridiculous. Saturday night can be your night to howl. Us old folks will just sit at home and read."

Laughter all around. The three headed to the house for showers and drinks before dinner. Cleaned and slightly greased was the only way. Food fine. Company quiet. Bed linen cool. Sleep deep. Morning sun awakened. Coffee stimulated. The two males settled in the sunroom.

"I spoke to my associates last evening. I've got some odd news and some odder news. First the odd: NeoBio Analysis ran tests on semen and hair. That's conclusive. The DNA from one matched the other. There is no cross-matched report. There are two reports based on two analyses. Unfortunately, the file copies of the reports and the retained samples of material can't be found. The lab techie thinks the police have them. The analysis went outside the normal loop of the ME's office because the police ordered it. They ordered it, so they say, to supplement the work of Dr. Minnig. I believe they ran the tests to get their own version of the truth. Now we have to scramble because the evidence to corroborate this point in our favor will be missing. We must be able to create confusion around the two tests. Tainted results and all that sort of stuff. That will be easy given the way the entire process was handled. Okay, we know which way to go. What we don't know is how your semen got to the scenes. That question has yet to be answered. Given the odder news, I know how I will proceed."

"What is the odder news?"

The trembling in Tony's voice said it all. He felt the shadows were gone and the evil was about to reveal itself. Sweat from the coffee, the sun, and his anxiety was making large semi-circles under his arms.

"I took the liberty of sending Connie's fingerprints—don't ask how I got them—to my friend at the FBI. She was able to make a partial match to a young woman who at one time claimed to be the lover of Sonny 'The Gouger' Gentile. The young woman's name at the time was Maria Angelica Benedetto. She went by the street name of Mollie Bennett. When Mollie's or Maria's prints were taken, she was eighteen. She had been set-up in a midtown Manhattan Brownstone by Sonny, unbeknownst to his wife. Sonny was banging sisters. Before she was Sonny's mistress, Maria had had several arrests for possession and distribution of drugs, dating back to her fourteenth birthday. She was also arrested for extortion. She ran a street gang, which offered protection to local merchants.

"Sonny was ordered to get rid of her by his father in law, Anthony 'The Basher.' It seems Anthony's older daughter complained to Daddy. And she meant more to Anthony than Sonny did. What happened to Mollie after she was thrown out of her palace of pleasure is anybody's guess. She simply went under the water. Now she has breached into your life."

"Not much of what you can tell me shocks me anymore. I am numb to all the half-truths, lies, and innuendoes. You said the FBI was able to match a partial."

"Actually, three partials."

"How reliable is the match?"

"As of now, less than forty percent. There appears to be significant damage to the fingers which left the prints. Almost as if the owner wanted to destroy a traceable identity. Acid and amateur surgeries are the guesses of the FBI. I say, as of now, because with more lab work, they hope to increase the reliability factor to sixty or seventy-five percent. This will take three to five days. All the work has to be done as a favor to me. I will owe a big-time quo for my friend's quid, assuming the match is on the money. Then we will know that she is the link to the crimes. Here's a possible sequence of events. SIU begins to feel the heat from the DA's office. They have to be sensitive to that. They deflect as much of the heat as possible to Gentile and Benedetto. The two thugs come up with a plan. Hire someone to sweep away the debris.

They decide the biggest pieces of debris are Washington, Mirtan, and you. What better way to frighten three birds with one stone than to kill a link connecting them? This murder also gets you involved, particularly when SIU sic two of their own on your ass. That I understand. Killing Magee confirms you as the murderer. Kelly and Echlebaum were waiting for you to arrive at Magee's. They had been tipped off by someone at SIU, who had been tipped off by Sonny, who had been tipped off by Connie or Mollie or Maria, whatever her name is. What I don't understand is how Charlotte Jenks fits into all this."

"Whoa, I'm supposed to accept that the woman I love and am planning to marry is a former teenage junkie, hooker, and mob mistress based upon a less than fifty/fifty shot that her fingerprints match some FBI files, to which you and I have no access. I am supposed to accept that best case scenario is that after a week the odds will skyrocket to two-in-three. Odds, which will fail in court. I'm supposed to accept that this woman has changed her identity and works for the mob at the behest of the SIU. I'm supposed to accept that this woman is schooled in a particularly vicious method of killing, which she learned somewhere. I'm supposed to believe that she has been lying to me. That she doesn't love me. That she wants me to die for her crimes. That she is so berserk, she killed one too many people in her efforts to convince the authorities that I was the murder. I say bullshit."

"You say bullshit. But as your lawyer, your defender, I say it provides us a credible avenue of escape from these charges, if we can get hard evidence."

"You're asking me to throw my affianced to the wolves, to save myself, based on a 'maybe' from the feds, whom I never trusted anyway. No can do."

"I'm not asking you to do anything. I'm telling you a direction I think has viability. A direction to save you from the long rest. You may choose to not consider this an option, but I do."

"I hired you, I can fire you."

"True, but that would not stop me from going to the DA with the knowledge I have. As an officer of the court, I am bound to be forthcoming with any information pertinent to the case."

"Great, what are my choices? Be convicted and die alone in prison or deflect the DA's attack to my beloved, have her convicted, and live alone like a pariah in public life. Suppose you and the feds are very wrong? A true case of mistaken identity. And you deflect everything onto her. The bad guys will support anything you want from them just to lighten their load. She becomes the patsy for the murders, because of a very unsavory past. She meets the sticker man, and I lose again. This is great."

"Hard evidence would confirm or refute this avenue."

"I will not be a party to this witch hunt."

"You don't have to be. But we need to be prepared for Monday's meeting with Ms. Nunno. I'll handle it."

Tony was fraught with anxiety. His gut reaction was to run to Connie and ask her directly. No secrets. But his faith in their relationship—or his hope in their relationship—whispered that this all would blow over like an afternoon shower. A different feeling than fright. Confusing facts and conflicting emotions. Great. Now all he could do is sit tight and pretend that nothing was wrong, nothing was wrong, nothing was wrong. The afternoon unfolded into a full thirty-six hours. Evening and the traditional cocktails: blessed relief to the tedium of no time passing. He and Connie planned a steak, corn on the cob, and baked potato on the grill.

Franklin decided to begin his venture into the singles' world at the Beach Comber hotel. The slightly dog-eared bastion of two-and-three-day stays has a HIS—Hooray It's Saturday—Party, featuring a nondescript island band, extensive free buffet, and expensive watered-down sweet cocktails. The demographic profile of the attendees was forty-plus, formerly married, and "Looking for Love in all the Wrong Places." Ideal for a looking loner like Franklin.

Connie smiled at Tony and asked a regular question. "How long will the potatoes take on the grill?"

"You always ask that question, and you always get the same answer: ninety minutes. The corn will take twenty minutes. And the steak will take a total of thirteen minutes: three, three, five, and two minutes. If the coals are hot enough to start now, dinner should be ready at eight."

Connie had her answers. "You're the chef and maid tonight. I want a nap. I'll be down to dine. Can you handle the pressure of preparation all by yourself?"

"Yes, dear."

⁀ↄↃↄ

The Beach Comber had seen better days, but so had Franklin. The young woman at the desk exchanged a buffet ticket for the price of two drinks. Fifteen dollars meant that the buffet was not really free. The steel drum sounds of "de Island, man" were emanating from pool side. The crowd was milling, noshing, and drinking. In reality, they were scoping out candidates for possible "amour du noir."

There was the normal quota of lounge lizards and tired, yet hopeful, females. Guys with gold chains. Guys with bad hairpieces. Guys with white leather slip-ons. Women with too much make up. Women whose very dark brown, leathery flesh sagged. A lot of ill-fitting, too-tight clothing in gaudy colors. Was Franklin just another clown in the circus? The bar had no Balvenie, so Franklin ordered scotch in a tall glass with lots of ice. He took a sip. Barely acceptable. He planned to nurse his two or three drinks so that conquest before slumber was possible.

Slightly greased, not non-functional, he headed for the far side of the pool. He could watch the entire area and particularly anyone who entered.

⁀ↄↃↄ

At the beach house, with any kind of good luck, Tony Could drink himself into a stupor so that he did not have to rationally deal with Connie until Sunday when Franklin was there. Another drink. Another sunset. The end of another disorienting day. Balvenie gently dulled the senses. The drinker didn't feel drunk. It was just that, after four or five pours, arms and legs ceased to function in a normal and anticipated manner.

Connie's presence was felt before Tony saw her. She was drop-dead gorgeous. One of his shirts was open from the neck to below her breasts. The shirt was knotted in front. Her bronzed and rigid midriff was bare beneath the big knot. Shorts that gave new meaning to the word short. Perhaps they should be called skimpies. Drink in hand, she announced her arrival.

"Hey there, stranger, would you like company for dinner. And, maybe after dinner, you'd like to party hearty. Seriously, is there anything I can do to help?"

"Nope. The food should be ready in about ten minutes. And, I got lit about an hour after the fire did. I see you have decided to join me in the euphoria of Balvenie."

"I come prepared."

As he headed for the grill, Tony's steps were slow and unsure, and his hands responded as if they were encased in lead. His mind was not as dull as his physicality, and he was enduring a rush of pure paranoia. His defensive senses were tingling. He was acutely alert to the presence of life-threatening danger. The rabbit tried to make no sudden moves, while the hunter circled centimeters closer to his trophy. The rabbit was trapped between the hunter and some barrier, like a wall. Tonight, the shoreline was the barrier, and Tony had to move and be functionally human. Plates were loaded and placed on the mats on the canopied table. The rabbit and hunter enjoyed a hearty last supper. Too much food. Belly over-stuffed. It was as if he had not eaten in days before tonight and would not eat again for three or four more days. Or ever. Did he store-up for a long journey? Like to eternity. Muscles were taught with discomfort. Clean up was arduous. With substantial and rapid intakes of food, the blood rushed to the stomach to facilitate the digestive process. Given the limited amount of blood within the body and the hammering effects of the Scotch whiskey, the digestive process caused great and widespread fatigue in areas outside the stomach. It was tiring for Tony to stand at the sink and clean the dinner service. He was vulnerable, and he knew it. It was more than a feeling. It was fact.

Connie got up from the table. "I'm going upstairs to freshen up. I'll be back in a few minutes, looking for my party animal."

Clean up complete, Tony retreated to the chaise lounge on the back deck. His drink in hand, he plopped on the cushion, exhaled, and stared out at the black sea accented by white crests. The booze and food caused his eyelids to become heavy. Not sleep, as much as relief from the tension of the past weeks.

"Hello, sailor."

Connie returned for her sexual conquest. She was wearing an XXL T-shirt and thong. Clutching her small bag by her side, as if to hide it, she effortlessly and quietly slid to Tony's side, leaned over, and kissed him deeply. He was not asleep yet. She raised the T and lowered her breasts to Tony's face. Rubbing them from side to side caused her breathing to slow down and become deeper. Excitement was visible via her nipples.

"Let's have a nightcap and play out here. Hand me your glass, I'll fetch."

ເນເ

Back at the Beach Comber, Franklin was not sure the band was any good. They all sounded alike. Fun for a while, but not acceptable as a steady musical diet. He had seen two possibilities. One raven-tressed and one toasted almond. They were not together, although the thought of that intrigued him. Raven looked to be mid-forties. Toasted almond was about ten years younger. Raven had the allure of a siren—seductive and destructive. Toasted almond gave off the aura that she would make Franklin breakfast the morning after. His target decision is made for him as he watches toasted almond embrace another woman and run her tongue along the interloper's neck and into her ear. Raven, it was then.

As he gulped down his drink for courage, raven's eyes spied Franklin looking at her. She was standing near, but not talking to two other women and an older man. She smiled at Franklin and nodded at his gaze. He strode to her side, as if he had known her all his life. Pure false bravado. He took her by the arm, and they walked to the steps leading to the beach. They were in synch. It was as if they had done this together many times before. This was magic. At the water's edge, he introduced himself and learned that she was Pamela Jackson. Franklin, strangely at ease, told her his name and how nervous he was at approaching her. Her skin was tan and her body intoxicatingly fragrant. Pam's smile dispelled all misconceptions about sirens. She was nervous, too. But she was glad he came over to her. The waves seemed to create a sound barrier. Their whispering was theirs alone to share.

❦❧❦

At the beach house, Connie handed Tony a drink. "Here you go. The last tall one. Now, where were we?"

He gulped deeply, as Connie slid down to his face and reintroduced her breasts to his mouth. She pulled away ever so slightly to let him take a big drink. Tony swallowed two mouths full of the elixir. Connie began to kiss his face and neck as her hands traversed his chest and stomach to his waist. Drinking and kissing. Licking and sipping. Inhaling body warmth and swallowing exchanged saliva. She tugged at the Velcro fly flap and unlaced through the eyelets. The coolness of her hands was lost in the warmth of his penis and scrotum. Tony hooked his fingers on her thong and pulled the meager vestige of modesty to the floor. As Connie stepped out of the black thong, she lowered herself to his readiness. She took him in her mouth and, holding the shaft with one hand, delicately ran the fingers of her other hand around and over his scrotum. He kicked his pants off and spreads his legs to provide her complete access. She took everything. He faded from the space they occupied.

Physically he was there. It was as if he had gone deep into the shadowy world of himself. He could see, hear, and feel what was happening. The intense pleasure was not lost on Tony. It was just that he couldn't respond to it. Booze and resignation had taken over. Connie raised her head and set herself astride him. She guided his entry. The strokes were shallow and hesitant at first but grew deeper and deeper gradually as natural lubricant allowed. He craved the warmth inside but could do nothing. He was an inert part of the process, just as if he were a battery-less vibrator. With her feet on the deck, she was completely impaled. Connie bounced up and down. With each complete cycle, her pleasure mounted. Her breathing was in rhythm with her bouncing. She began to toss her hair and dug her nails into Tony's chest. He felt pain, pleasurable pain, but could not react to respond. Pain reminded him he was alive.

∽∾∽

On the beach, Pam said she was afraid and embarrassed to come to The Beach Comber. She talked incessantly, as if talking were a way to rid her of nervousness. Yes, she knew it was a meeting hall. She wanted to meet people—men. But something in her past told her that nice girls didn't go to places like this and make themselves available to strangers. Everyone was a stranger until they were introduced. She had been divorced for four years. Her children were in college. She was a manager of a bank's branch office in Conshohocken, west of Philly. She wanted another drink. They walked to the beach side of the bar, and he bought her a Long Island Ice Tea—a scotch for him. She took two big pulls on her drink. Alcohol aided in the release of her anxiety. Franklin told her about his recent life—leaving out the entire present situation. He had two pairs of shoes slung over his shoulders as they walked along the surf, holding hands. They traveled about one hundred yards away from the hotel's deck and made the turn.

They were face to face. He dropped the shoes, slipped his arm behind her, and drew her body to his. She raised her face and kissed him before he could initiate the act. She clutched him. He hugged her strongly. The kiss seemed to last two minutes. Each time one of them pulled away slightly, the other gently rubbed lips, and they returned to real kissing. Tongues began to dart in and out. Nothing sloppy. Just exploratory. Finally, she retreated and rested her head on his shoulder. She was sighing. She attacked his neck and right earlobe. Ever so slightly, he applied pressure at the hip. She settled in on his thigh and returned the pressure. His thigh made a gradual circular motion, and she reciprocated. The two bodies were delicately undulating. She raised her head again and attached her lips to his. She had moved her hips to the front and was now grinding in an upward motion. His arousal was teenage—awkwardly obvious.

⌘

At the beach house, Connie's bouncing began to

slow. She raised her hips to the point just before complete extraction. She then slid down the pole completely. Her chamber seemed to swallow all of Tony. He could do nothing. The stupor was total. She was using him as she wished—for her singular enjoyment. To prolong her pleasure, she rested at the nadir of the cycle. She looked at Tony. There was nothing soft or loving in her eyes. The demonic presence was visible. She reached into the clutch purse and withdrew a large lipstick case.

"I'll bet you and your nosy friend would like to have found this a few weeks ago."

With her left hand, she removed the tube's outer sleeve, which she screwed to the bottom of the inner portion. Then she gave the outer sleeve a twist, and the pick popped out. A twist back and the pick was locked in place. A clutch-purse-sized dagger. Just what the well-dressed murderess was carrying these days.

"I heard you two yammering, and I know that you know who I am and what I have done. So now I have to do you and Franklin the Jerk. But I thought that before I did you, I would do you. How wonderfully ironic is that? When it is all over, your bodies will be out at sea. And there is nothing you can do about it. I laced your drink. A spoon full and the date is out cold. But a few drops of GHB, coupled with the booze, render the victim—that's you—helpless. You can see what will happen. You can feel the ice pick's insertion. You can taste your own blood. But you can't do jack shit to stop me. And, when your dying body slowly drifts out to sea to become fish food, you will sense your own drowning. Hell, the authorities won't even find pieces. I'll ice your lawyer, the late-night lothario. And, if he got lucky, I'll do his paramour. Her body will remain as part of the house. It'll look like you killed once again and split. I've got tape, a cigarette butt, and your semen from the condom you are wearing. Everything you needed to see and understand was in my leather bag in our walk-in closet at home. Right under your nose. You are such an asshole. But you served a purpose, so I don't really hate you. Now you're baggage. You know the Latin word for baggage. It's *impedimenta.* You are truly an impediment. Enough chit-chat, I want to get off. So I will go bouncy, bouncy up and down."

ശ്ശേ

On the beach, Pam and Franklin's kisses had gone from passionate, hard, bone-to-bone attacks to slow and tender expressions of emotions long-pent-up deep. Shoes were on the sand. Drink cups were on the sand. Hands traced contours. Fingers dug and massaged. Two torsos had become a single entity. They separated to steady themselves against the tips of the waves and the softening sand. They caught their respective breaths. Pam's smile and the tears flowing down her cheeks were highlighted by the lights from the hotel deck. She began to giggle.

"I haven't made any female giggle from one of my kisses since Susie Winters, and that was when I was ten. Have I done anything to offend you, Pam?"

"On the contrary. I haven't felt the pleasure of a kiss

in twelve years. Yes, that includes the last years of my marriage. I feel like a teenager all over again. It feels nice, so I feel naughty. My heart rate is at least one hundred, and I am having difficult time breathing. These are signs of a stroke or the precursors to rapture. I opt for rapture. And, I can feel you do also. Now the question is how to resolve the dilemma of emotions and locale. I don't want to do what I want to do here in the sand before the watchful eyes of sixty strangers."

"We can go to my place. Actually, it's not my place. I'm a weekend guest. I left my hosts at home to dine alone. Before I left, they were starting the wassailing. By now they are drunk and in bed. A place I would like to be as soon as possible with you."

"Lead on."

They headed onto the deck, through the hotel lobby and to the parking lot. Tony's Mazda awaited. Franklin unlocked the passenger side door and opened it for Pam. As she settled into the seat, she reached up, unzipped his fly, and took a firm grip on his tumescent penis. Soft strokes created a full erection. She kissed it. His instinct was to lean into the car and let her finish what she had started, but she pushed him out onto the tarmac and closed the door.

Franklin had to walk around the back of the car, put his erection back inside his shorts, and zip up without be-ing a spectacle in front of the couples who were entering cars nearby. He grinned. This was more fun than he could have imagined.

❧

Connie's moaning had reached a crescendo, and the sexual pulsation was permeating her entire body—chest, thighs, legs, and arms. When the tremors died down, she took Tony's drink and poured a little more into his mouth. He coughed because swallowing was a voluntary action. Connie stepped off her saddle and viciously pounded Tony to climax. Much like getting sperm from a bull. No emotion and no pleasure. She removed the condom and inverted its contents into a small vial, which she took to the kitchen freezer. She might need Tony's essence later. She re-dressed in her thong and T-shirt. Returning to the chaise lounge, she smiled at her comatose, non-feeling former lover.

"It's time to rid myself of the *impedimenta*. You're going for a swim. Well, not really a swim. You're going for a drowning."

She rolled Tony on his side, put one arm at his knees, and her other arm at his armpits. She hoisted him up, eased him over her shoulder, and headed to the shoreline. His lack of comfort was of no concern to her. The sand was soft and made every heavy step precarious. Twice Connie almost fell, but her years at The Seven Sisters had made her strong enough to carry this load. The tide was going out. She waded out to where the water was waist deep. The outward tug of the current confirmed the wisdom of her timing. The baggage plopped into the water. A wave lifted them both up then back down where she could stand. Tony's eyes were wide open. Fear spoke for him. He couldn't even blink. He saw the darkness of the night. He was comatose. She took the pick from the waistband of her thong and grabbed a hand full of Tony's hair. Raising his head and pushing it back exposed the pick's target.

"You wanna know why the three? I'll tell ya. Charlotte was for practice. I hadn't been asked to do somebody since that grab-ass mick captain out on Long Island Sound. Chakika was for pay. I got fifty thousand dollars for that job. Detective Myers was personal. I knew she was after your ass and the rest of you. I couldn't be uncovered just because you decided to follow your little head. I was waiting at her place and entered when you left that night. She opened the door, thinking I was you. The rest was easy. You can find the cigarette butts all over the street. But, who cares about the finer points of my craft. Bye-bye asshole."

☙❧

Franklin and Pam were locked in a crouch-groping embrace in the front seat of Tony's car parked underneath the big pine tree. They were wrestling with each other's clothing and the clothing was winning. There simply was not enough room in the front seat for two adults to undress each other while feverishly sucking on body parts. Time for rationally thinking people to exit the auto and rush to a bedroom so that this act of youthful exuberance could be consummated. Franklin didn't even bother to lock the doors. They entered the house and peered into the living room, the sunroom, and onto the deck. There were Tony's pants and a small black clutch purse.

"Have they gone to bed?"

"Dunno. Stay here, let me look upstairs."

Franklin looked through the open door of Tony's bedroom. No bodies and no noise from the bathroom. There on the bed was a leather bag. Its contents were strewn over the spread. Two rolls of duct tape and a knife. A box of roofing nails and a small hammer. A six-pack of condoms and two glass vials. One empty and one containing a clear liquid. The Handyman's toolkit. Franklin bounded down the stairs and rushed to the deck. From there, he spied Connie coming up the small boardwalk from the beach. Her giant T-shirt is sopping wet from her breasts down. He noticed a glint of light from her right hand.

"Pam, grab a phone and call nine-one-one. Tell them we have a homicide at Forty-Three Ocean Drive. Tell them the murderer is trying to escape."

"What the hell is going on here?"

"I can't explain now, but you've got to trust me. This is a very bad situation. I think a friend of mine, Tony, has just been killed and his murderer is about to join us on the deck to continue her evening's work. You and I are most likely next on her hit list. Now, please call the police."

Pam seized a phone from the counter as Connie climbed the stairs to the deck.

"Okay, Connie or Mollie or Maria, what have you done with Tony?"

"To use a hackneyed phrase, he sleeps with the fish-es. Now it's your turn. Hey, I see your trolling was successful. And, the dumb bitch will make four. Tony will be good to the last drop. Your girlfriend will be found just as the others. The police will conclude that you and Tony escaped."

Connie lunged at Franklin, and the ice pick pierced his left side. The impact of her blow caused him to double over and forced his wind from him. She was strong, and her purpose was clear. As he rose, gasping for breath, he locked his right hand onto the front of Connie's throat. His thumb was on one side of her windpipe, his index and middle fingers were on the other. The pressure he applied emanates from the fear of death. He was holding on for dear life. His. She was caught in a vise. As he tried to lift her from the deck, Franklin pushed his hand upward, increasing the pressure on her neck and seriously impeding her ability to breathe. Her victim's reaction and action confirmed the magnitude of the struggle. He would not go quietly into the good night. Groping for the pick, she slapped at his torso and tried to retrieve the pick. He turned so that she couldn't reach the dirk's handle, but he never let loose his grip. To do so would be the end of the battle and his life.

The pain in his stomach was now spreading through his body. He was beginning to become disoriented. The harder he squeezed, the more he hurt. The more he hurt, the more disoriented he became. The more disoriented he became, the more he had to squeeze just to remain conscious, to remain focused on self-defense. Connie's eyes were wide open with fear and rage. She was prepared to fight for her life and take his. She kicked at Franklin's gut and his balls. More pain. She punched his face. These were not the slaps of a woman, but the rights and lefts of a prizefighter. More pain for Franklin. More pressure on Connie's breathing tube. She began to spit and cough. She was running dangerously low on oxygen. The spit in the corner of her mouth had turned white. As he drew his free hand back to punch her, he heard a *thunk*. Connie grunted. Her offensive activity froze. And she blinked. Then the second *thunk*. Pam had hit Connie on the back of her skull with the large thick kitchen carving board. The sound of the object striking a skull was like no other. Sickening and dull. The three-inch-thick, eighteen-inch-square kitchen utensil had been put to a new use. It was a weapon of liberation.

Pam delivered three solid blows to the back of Connie's head. The last one with the edge of the board was superfluous.

Connie's eyes were all white, and the irises had rolled back. Now her eyes closed. She went limp, and Franklin was left holding the prize above his head. He loosened his grip, and she cascaded to the floor. His fingers hurt more than his gut.

"Are you all right?" Pam asked. "Look at the blood. Can you breathe? Who is she? Why was she attacking you? What have I done?"

"I've got to find Tony. I need more help from you. He is probably in the water. I need you to stay here and wait for the police. Watch Connie. Here's my card. When the cops come, tell them that Connie tried to kill me, that she is the Handyman Killer wanted in New York, and that I am in the water looking for Tony Sattill. Now we have to find a big flashlight. If you were a flashlight, where would you be?"

"I'd be in the kitchen. In a drawer or in a small closet, depending on the size."

The two wannabe-copulators rushed to the kitchen and frantically searched for a flashlight.

"Here it is," Pam call out. "In the closet with the brooms and mops. And it's a big one. Best of all, the light works."

Pam handed the booty to Franklin. She couldn't help but stare at the large bloodstain surrounding the silver handle stuck in his gut.

"Are you strong enough to look for your friend? Before you go anywhere, tell me what the hell is going on here."

"No time for details, so here is the abridged version. My friend and client is Tony Sattill, a New York police detective accused of being the Handyman Killer. Maybe you've heard about the killer. But, as it has turns out, the real killer is the deep sleeper on the deck. The woman you just introduced to a new joy of cooking. Her real name is Benedetto, although she goes by the name Wilhaus. She is the daughter of a Long Island mob boss who has been under investigation for corruption and fraud. Tony and I recently uncovered exactly who the woman is and why she is the killer. I realize that is a lot to accept on faith or just my say so. I implore you to do as I ask. I think she has dumped Tony in the ocean. Now I must find him. Will you do as I ask?"

"What choice do I have? Of course, I'll help."

As Franklin headed out to the deck, he heard the sirens. Soon he would have help. Soon Pam would have to explain the inexplicable. He carefully followed Connie's wet footsteps backward into the ocean where she deposited her former lover. Franklin fanned the light in search of a body. He saw nothing but black water and white foam. No full moon. Only the large flashlight. He was fearful about wading into the water. How deep was it? What was the bottom like? What was swimming and feeding near the shore? But he had no choice. He had to enter the unknown to save his friend. When he stepped waist deep into the cool water, he realized that he still hurt from the stab wound. Would the blood attract some really big feeders? What else could he do?

"Tony. Can you hear me? If you're out here, tell me where. Hang on, Tony, I'm coming."

Franklin saw nobody. He waded into the water. As he waded deeper, up to his armpits, he heard the commotion of male voices and saw the beams of light from behind him on the beach.

"Sir, stop where you are. We are the police. Stop where you are."

Franklin turned. "If you want me, you'll have to come down and get me and my pal."

"Sir, please stop and come to us with your hands over your head."

"Listen, you guys, the blonde you found on the deck just tried to kill New York City Police Detective Anthony Sattill. She stabbed him in the neck with a silver ice pick, which is now embedded in my gut. She dumped his body in the ocean. I need your help to find Tony. I hate the ocean and have no idea how or where to look."

"Okay, sir, we'll come out there and help you look. There's a sandbar about thirty yards out. If you get there, maybe you can see better."

Franklin was joined by two men in white-short sleeved shirts and blue shorts. The three of them waded out to sea. The sandbar rose mysteriously from the gully before it. Franklin was now shin deep in crashing water. The tide was pulling him. He hated this. The three of them turned their flashlights into shore. Three beacons. Three sweeps.

"There he is."

The two cops were running to a mass of pale ten yards to the left of Franklin. The sandbar appeared to have snagged Tony as it would a piece of driftwood. The cops retrieved Tony and hoisted him onto their shoulders for the trip to the water's edge. Franklin felt faint, but he couldn't sit down until he was on land. With ever-weakening steps, he headed against the tide to safety. Pam was waiting.

"I have a lot of explaining, but it will have to wait until after the local police have taken us all to the hospital. Please be patient, Pam."

Suddenly the world around Franklin faded to black. His head weighed a ton. He had no strength. He sat and then collapsed.

"Can somebody help me over here? This man is seriously hurt."

A paramedic left Tony and administered to Franklin.

Another paramedic arrived with a flat stretcher. The EMS vehicle was backing on to the beach. Franklin's eyes were closed, and his breathing was negligible.

The cops found the leather bag and all its contents, less the ice pick, next to the lounge chair. They got the ice pick from Franklin at the hospital. Everything was now under lock and key in the evidence cage.

The Coast Regional Medical Center had three new guests. The boys in one room and the girl in another. Each door had a police guard. Franklin had suffered extensive bleeding, but no damage to any internal organs. Transfusions, antibiotics, monitoring, and bed rest would heal the patient. Tony was in stable, but guarded, condition. He lost blood and swallowed some seawater. He was hooked up to tubes. He would be fine and was already moving his hands and blinking. Connie was very still, and the monitors were never changing. The trauma to the head caused by numerous blows from the three-inch-thick cutting board, along with the lack of oxygen from Franklin's hand on her throat, rendered her a vegetable, at least temporarily. She did not blink or react to stimuli. The doctors said it was too early for them to offer a prognosis. They'd have a better idea in a few days.

The state and local police were questioning Pam as if she knew everything that transpired that evening. They got very little. From Franklin, they got the name of New York Assistant Das, Marshall and Nunno, and Captain Brainerd of the NYPD. These stalwarts confirmed his story.

There was nothing more that could be done by Franklin or Tony until they returned to New York. Further efforts were in the capable hands of other authorities. There would be jurisdictional battles over where Connie got prosecuted first—if she recovered. However these were resolved, it would not be in her favor.

In the middle of some eternal baseball game, Pam entered Franklin's room. She had been allowed to go to her house and change her clothes. Her return to the hospital was strictly voluntary.

"Well, hello," she said. "You're awake. How do you feel? How do I feel? Fine, and thanks for asking. How does Tony feel? Don't stop me, I'm on a roll. I want you to know that last night was the most exciting date I've ever had. How often does a girl get involved in two attempted murders and get to come to the rescue of a stranger, who may or may not be a villain, in one night? Hell, in one lifetime. No need to explain now. I'll just accept the fact that you guys from New York live more interesting lives than we female divorced bankers from Philly. So here is the deal. I'm going to go home to the 'burbs and try not to think about what happened last night. I'll think about important issues like making sure we have enough deposit slips at the tables, and what I'll wear to the patio-pool party next week. You'll return to New York, heal and try to resolve petty issues like murder, corruption, and attempted murder. I'm sure I will be asked to give further testimony. I may even be called to New York. When I am, I will let you put me up at a nice hotel, and we can restart this relationship. And, maybe, just maybe, if your explanation of everything that has transpired during the past twenty-four hours makes sense, and you are very contrite about causing me great mental anguish, I will let you take me to the Caribbean for a week in February."

Her entire monologue lasted ten seconds. The reproach erupted from Pam as if it were all one word. She leaned over the bed and kissed Franklin tenderly on the lips. Then she gracefully twirled and sashayed out the door and into Franklin's future.

A double date in the Caribbean with a new-found friend, a savior, and cousin, Marie

About the Author

John Andes was born and raised in Central Pennsylvania and received a degree in philosophy from Brown University. His business career, centered on advertising and marketing, started in New York and moved to various cities in the US. He has written the entire spectrum of B2B and B2C marketing communications. Andes has two adult sons, is retired, and lives on the Florida Gulf Coast. He coaches little league football, mentors small business owners and entrepreneurs, and teaches creative writing. Andes has authored *Farmer in the Tal*, *Suffer the Children*, *Icarus*, *Matryoshka*, *Jacob's Ladder*, *Loose Ends*, *Control is Jack*, *Revenge*, *Adventures in House Sitting*, *Skull Stacker*, *Street Cleaners*, and *Question Everything...Then Dig Deeper*.

His web page is www.crimenovelsonline.com